ERLEND LOE is a Norwegian novelist.
His eight books have been translated
into over twenty languages.

DON BARTLETT lives in Norfolk, and
is the translator of, among others,
Per Petterson and Jo Nesbø.

DON SHAW lives in Denmark
and is the compiler of the standard
Danish-Thai dictionaries. They have
previously collaborated on novels by
Roy Jacobsen and Jakob Ejersbo.

Also by Erlend Loe

DOPPLER

Lazy Days

ERLEND LOE

Translated from the Norwegian by
Don Bartlett and Don Shaw

First published in the UK in 2013 by Head of Zeus Ltd.

Published in agreement with Rogers, Coleridge & White Ltd.,
20 Powis Mews, London W11 1JN, in association with Cappelen Damm AS,
Akersgata 47/49, Oslo, Norway

This translation has been published with the financial support of NORLA.

9 7 5 3 1 2 4 6 8

A CIP catalogue record for this book is available from the British Library.

ISBN (HB): 9781781855171
ISBN (eBook): 9781781855164

Typeset by www.BenStudios.co.uk

Printed in Germany.

Head of Zeus Ltd
Clerkenwell House
45–47 Clerkenwell Green
London EC1R 0HT

www.headofzeus.com

(Unfortunately a small dog was hurt while I was working on this book, but it received treatment fairly quickly and is now doing well, all things considered.)

Dear Angela & Helmut Bader
We are a family with three kids (5, 8
and 14 years) who are planning a holiday
in Garmisch-Partenkirchen, and we saw
your holiday house on the internet. We
plan to arrive on the 30th of June and
would like to stay until the first of
August. Is the house available in this
period (or close to it) and what is the
price? We are looking forward to your
answer.
Yours sincerely
Nina Telemann, with family

Hello Telemann available yes the price
65 Euro pro night, the children for free
I know your Imail unfortunately do not
read backwards to write it me please on
English Yours sincerely Fam Bader

Hello Fam Bader. We did not totally understand your last e-mail, but we are interested in renting the house. How should we pay you?
Nina Telemann

Hello Fam. Thank you for your Imail It
makes us happy you by 1. july to remain
wants. Our address reads Helmut and
Angela Bader Ludwigstrasse 5, Mixing
Part Churches. Our bank account: District savings
bank mixing part churches Big Byladem 1
gap iban/de xxxxxxxxxxxxxxxxx. We are
pleased also you and wish you up to then
a beautiful time. Fam Bader

Hello again. We have now paid the
deposit. The payment was made from my
husband's account. His name is Telemann.
We and our children are looking forward
to staying in your house. Do we go
straight to the house or should we
contact you somewhere else? We are not
sure yet about what time we will arrive
on first of july, but if you need to
know you could perhaps give us a phone
number so that we can send you an SMS or
call you.

Nina Telemann

Hello Fam Telemann Thank you for your
Imail They come on Wednesday to us to
mixing part churches. They can drive directly to
the holiday house, we live directly
beside it. Here they get then the keys.
Can they say to us when you approx in
mix will arrive? None should be at home,
call the Handyno. xxxxxxxxxxxx. We look
forward to you. Large Fam Bader

Do you have to smoke in here?

Yes.

But the weather's so nice outside.

Darling, it might not have occurred to you, but here we are on holiday in Germany yet again, a country you adore but which I don't, and this time, would you believe it, you have brought us to the very cradle of Nazism, and in return the deal is that I can smoke wherever I want.

Not in the car.

No, not in the car. But we're not in the car now, are we.

I don't know how the Baders would feel about you smoking in their house.

Do you mean Large Fam Bader?

Stop it, will you. They must have written Grüsse, which means 'Kind regards', and the translation software changed it to 'Large', but the family isn't large, there's just the two of them, and actually I think she's rather upset that they don't have any children.

What makes you think that?

You sense that sort of thing.

I think it's just as well. Horror of horrors, imagine

growing up in Mixing Part Churches.

The town isn't actually called Mixing Part Churches. And stop making fun of the translation software!

Don't you think it's funny that the Baders don't speak a word of English?

No, I don't.

Not even a bit funny?

No.

Not even the fact that they don't react to the software changing Garmisch-Partenkirchen to Mixing Part Churches?

No. And it's quite unreasonable of you to call this the cradle of Nazism.

I agree it's a little unreasonable, but it's not so wide of the mark.

There's not one German alive today responsible for what happened back then.

True enough.

Are you intending to smoke when the children come in?

Basically, yes.

Nina Telemann. 43 years old. Teacher of Norwegian at advanced level. Short-sighted. Glasses four centimetres thick. Well, one centimetre. But that's quite thick, too.

Bror Telemann. 42 years old. Stage director at the National Theatre.

Dreams of writing a play himself one day. A helluva good one. Which sets the standard. Excellent eyesight. Alcohol problems? Nooo. Not really.

Do you think Mixing Part Churches is the type of place people lock up their kids, or others' kids, in the cellar for twenty-four years and rape them three thousand times?

That's enough.

No, but do you think so?

Stop that now.

For Christ's sake, no harm speculating.

Stop it.

You don't think this is a hub for that sort of practice then?

No.

So, those things don't happen here?

I don't think so.

So, we just let the kids run about on their own?

I think so.

Good.

MIXING PART WILL TEAR us apart.

What did you say?

Nothing.

You said something. I heard it.

If you absolutely want to know I thought I was on my own, humming an old tune and without thinking I switched one word in the chorus to Mixing Part and that's about all there is to it.

Fine.

Actually, it happens quite a lot, I think I'm on my own in a room and then it turns out you're here, too. You're a quiet sort, you are.

So are you.

You mean we're both quiet sorts.

Yes.

Dɪᴅ ʏᴏᴜ ʙᴜʏ ᴀɴʏ red wine?

It's on the worktop in the kitchen.

But, darling, this is German wine.

I don't like you calling me 'darling'.

I thought we loved each other.

Of course we do.

So what's the problem?

You say 'darling' when you're annoyed, imagining that your on-the-surface friendly tone will give the impression that your aggression is subdued and under control. But the effect is quite the opposite. It has nothing to do with your love for me, even though you may think so.

I want wine, Nina, not a discussion about you and me.

The wine's on the worktop.

But this is German red wine.

Yes. So?

I can't drink German red wine.

Can't you?

No, I can't.

Why don't you open the bottle and try it?

No.

Why not?

Because I can't.

Alright. I still feel I've kept my end of the deal.

When does the Lidl in Olympiastrasse close?

No idea.

I thought you adored this country and had its customs down pat.

I do.

But you don't know when the Lidl in Olympiastrasse in Mixing Part Churches closes?

No, I don't. And it's not called Mixing Part Churches.

GOOD NIGHT.

Good night.

Bror?

Mhm?

I know it's a bit intimate and not something we normally talk about, but couldn't you tell me about one of your sexual fantasies?

No.

Go on.

Now, do you mean?

Yes.

No.

Why not?

I don't want to.

Do you think it's embarrassing?

No, not embarrassing exactly, but …

Come on.

I haven't got any.

What?

I haven't got any sexual fantasies.

Everybody has.

Not me.

Of course you have.

I haven't.

You used to have.

Used to, yes.

You've stopped having them then, have you?

Yes.

What do you think about then?

I don't know. All sorts of things. The theatre. Basically I think mostly about the theatre.

Do you never look at me and sort of undress me with your eyes if I'm standing in a sexy pose, for example.

Don't think so.

What about other women?

No. I think about the theatre.

What about Nigella?

I've never thought about her in that way.

Do you really mean that?

Yeah.

Telemann, you're beginning to worry me.

Oh yeah. Good night.

Now I *am* worried.

YOU'RE SO QUIET TODAY.

I thought you said we were both quiet sorts.

Yes, but today you're especially quiet. Is there something the matter?

I don't think so.

There is something the matter. What is it?

I don't know.

Is it what we were talking about last night?

No.

I bet it is.

I'm not thinking about what we talked about last night, Nina. I'm not.

What are you thinking about then?

I'm not sure. Theatre maybe.

Rubbish. You're not thinking about the theatre.

OK.

Do you want to tell me what you're actually thinking?

No.

Not at all?

No.

I've got to get to the bottom of this, Telemann. Sorry, but

now I really have to insist.

Right.

Is it about the play you want to write, but have never got going with, even though you claim to think about it all the time?

No.

Is it about me?

No

About the children?

No.

About Heidi? Are you annoyed because she plays so much tennis?

Good God no. She can play as much tennis as she wants – at any rate so long as she's fully aware it's you pushing her and not me.

I don't think I'm pushing her.

Are you kidding? You spend every minute buying sports gear and organising training sessions and competitions and diets.

But she wants to get to the top, doesn't she.

Yes, that's what she says. But where does this ambition come from, do you think?

Actually it was you we were talking about. We were saying you were particularly quiet, and I was trying to find out why. Is it something to do with Germany?

No.

Not at all?

No.

Not about Bavaria being the cradle of Nazism?

No.

OK, I give up.

Great.

Just a mo. Has it got anything to do with Nigella? You're not answering me, but I'm absolutely positive it's about Nigella. It's her, isn't it. I know it is. You don't need to say anything, Telemann, I can see it in your face.

Nina is right. Telemann is thinking about Nigella Lawson. He doesn't like to talk about this, but he thinks about her quite a lot.

It started when Nina bought him *Nigella Bites*, a cookery book, a birthday present. He thanked her politely, thinking that when you start giving each other cookery books the relationship is on its last legs, but he didn't say anything. On the contrary. Telemann has been good at receiving presents without revealing his disappointment ever since as a child he was given a weaving frame, and saw from his father's eyes that he and Mum had had a battle over this, and Dad must have lost and Mum was on tenterhooks, and Telemann didn't have the heart to disappoint her, so he thanked her warmly and wove all through the Christmas holiday. The whole point of presents, as Telemann understood it, lies in the bonds they create between the giver and the receiver, and as such presents have no inherent value. And, at first, he thought that *Nigella Bites* was just such a present. But, without knowing why, he carried on leafing through the book. He looked at recipes, photographs of food, as in all cookery books, and descriptions of what you have to do, but he also looked at the photographs of Nigella herself, taken while she was in the kitchen, bending over pots and pans, dressed in different outfits, sniffing at the ingredients, mixing, stirring, pouring, for example milk from one smallish bowl to a larger one, and putting things into her mouth or about to put things into her mouth. Sometimes her eyes are what could best be described as delectable; at others they are mischievous, cheeky even. When she is dressed in black she is slightly dangerous, someone a person like Telemann could never have approached or addressed, but when she is wearing that thin pale blue sweater of hers and holding, say, a dessert bowl of strawberries and cream in her left hand and a spoon in her right, her head slightly bowed, she is soft and almost vulnerable, and to all appearances in need of comfort from someone like Telemann.

Moreover, he thinks Nigella is fascinatingly well-built. She has, for instance, got hips. And a bosom.

I GOT TALKING TO a woman in Lidl's.

Crikey, did you now, Telemann?

Berthold and Sabine began to play with her kid and so I think she felt it would be only natural to say something.

What did she say?

She told me her name was Lisa and she was American. And then she went on about a fantastic castle that was supposed to be just like out of a fairy tale, breath-taking, by all accounts, and it is very near here.

It's called Neuschwanstein.

Really? And she went on and on about how she had pushed her boyfriend to come to Europe to see this castle, but he only wanted to go to Mexico and they had almost split up over it, but then she had dug her heels in and they had travelled to Germany and both of them had been blown away by this castle and he had proposed to her there and then and later they had a photo of the castle on the wedding invitations and of course they had a wedding cake made in the shape of the castle and now they have two children and usually come here every alternate summer.

Mhm.

We have so much fun in Europe, she said that several times.

Mhm.

I think I'll have to write that sentence down.

Do that.

I must do it before I forget it.

Are you thinking of using it in the play?

Possibly.

Terrific. Are you going to meet her again, or what?

I hardly think so.

GOD, THE BATTERY IN my toothbrush is flat again.

That's annoying

Annoying? It's useless. I only just bought it, you know.

You'll have to remember to charge it tonight.

I do every night.

Have you considered emailing Braun about it? I don't think they should be allowed to get away with selling us sub-standard products.

That's right. Can we do that? Do you think they'll answer?

Of course they will. For companies like them customer care is paramount. There'll be seven or eight of them sitting there, just waiting for your email, at this very moment.

Once a day Telemann goes to the bathroom and sits on the toilet for a long time. Not because he's constipated, but because he thinks it's good to sit alone and think about the theatre. He switches on Nina's toothbrush and lets it run down to time himself. He thinks he is entitled to the half an hour or so it takes for the battery to go flat. Telemann-time is how he thinks of it. Or theatre-time. The one merges into the other. It's not easy for an outsider to know where Telemann-time ends and theatre-time begins. Telemann doesn't even know himself. It's not so uncommon for him to think about the theatre so much that when the toothbrush stops whirring he forgets to put it back in the charger. It is left standing on the edge of the sink, run down and all alone.

TELEMANN! IS THERE SOMETHING wrong?

Eh? No, no, I was dreaming. It was just a dream.

What about?

Nothing important.

It must have been. Everything that happens to you is important to me.

Do you mean that?

Of course.

Wow.

Don't you feel that way about me?

Yes … yes I do, I just haven't put it into, what shall I say, such a clear formulation, sort of.

What were you dreaming about?

About Charles Saatchi, if you absolutely have to know.

Who's Charles Saatchi?

He's just a rich Englishman who was born into a Jewish family in Baghdad, but then they moved to London when he was four. I don't quite know why. Perhaps it wasn't so easy to be a Jew in Baghdad. Anyway, he started a large advertising agency with his brother and he also collects art.

Why did you dream about him?

I don't know.

What did you dream about then?

It was like a house, a really magnificent house, you know the kind of London house with white bricks and several storeys, and it was by a rectangular park surrounded by the same expensive houses, and I wanted so much to see into the house. I felt there was someone inside who wanted me to go in. But then Charles Saatchi blocked the way. He was standing right in front of the door smiling one of those affluent smiles that said I might as well forget all about going inside, I wouldn't be allowed in there in a thousand years, sort of, if you understand what I mean, that's what his smile said, and I was so angry, I told him to wipe that grin off his face, but he just stood there and stood there and I could see there was nothing I could do, and I was frustrated and fed up, but he just smiled all the more.

Golly. Yes, I can see how frustrating that must have been.

Yes, it was.

But you don't know why you dreamt about him?

Nope.

Do you know anything more about him?

Not really.

But still your subconscious churns round, feeling that he's some kind of threat?

Mhm.

Well, that's very strange.

Yes.

I think this is exciting, Telemann. Now let's do a bit more investigating.

OK.

Tell me more about him.

I don't know a lot more.

Has he got any hobbies?

Collecting art.

Yes, you said that. Is he married?

Eh, what?

I asked if he was married.

Err ... I can't remember.

Think your voice went a bit funny there.

I was just feeling tired.

OK. Shall we go back to sleep then?

If you like.

Good night.

Good night.

NINA DOESN'T KNOW, BUT Charles Saatchi is married to Nigella, and Telemann would be the first to admit that he has problems accepting that. He thinks about Saatchi almost as much as he does about Nigella. Often when the nice thoughts about Nigella have got a hold and Telemann is really enjoying himself, such as when he is in the kitchen making her food, then the nasty thought of Saatchi creeps into the picture. It doesn't push Nigella away completely but it merges with her and unnecessarily complicates and contaminates the moment. Once when Telemann was sitting on the sofa at home, thinking about the theatre, his thoughts turned to Nigella instead. He fetched his laptop, the one he primarily uses to note down ideas about plays, and searched for pictures of Nigella. He found a lot and spent a good, long time studying several of them. He wondered whether he dared to save a couple of them deep in the machine, but he didn't. After a while he came across a photograph of Nigella and Charles Saatchi sitting in a car, presumably a classic London taxi, Telemann thought. He had never seen a photo of Nigella with Saatchi before and the image upset and bothered him to such a degree that he couldn't think sensibly about the theatre for several days. It was a shock to see them together in a picture. Suddenly he realised that Nigella had entered the relationship voluntarily, of her own free will, fully aware of her actions, so to speak. Sitting there on the back seat, she is smiling, bedecked in rich, elegant apparel, with mauve sunglasses and matching shawl, over the black dress, and Saatchi is sitting beside her, not especially close, a fact that Telemann felt emphasises Saatchi's proprietary relationship towards her. His possession of her is so indisputable that he doesn't even need to sit close to her. From the moment Telemann saw this photograph a feeling of resentment grew inside him towards Charles Saatchi. To his wealth. To the damned secretiveness that surrounds him. To the fact that he never speaks to journalists. To his non-appearances at the opening of the art exhibitions he has himself organised. Even to the double 'a' in his name. The list of things about Saatchi that Telemann considers provocative is very long.

Nina came into the room as Telemann was studying the photograph and he reacted by quickly closing the laptop.

What was that?

Nothing.

Are you looking at porn?

No.

What are you doing then?

I'm thinking about the theatre.

And then you slam your laptop shut when I come into the room?

Yes.

Knowing that will make me suspicious?

Yes. But sometimes when you're thinking about the theatre you have to slam your laptop shut. That's the way it is.

DAD, WHAT'S REVOLTING MINUS one?

I think you should go back to sleep, Berthold.

Yes, but what is revolting minus one?

What it is? I … don't know. Actually it's an impossibility.

Typical of you, that is. You're incredibly bad at doing calculations with words.

You could be right. What's the answer?

The answer is the word that someone invented immediately before revolting.

And which word was that?

I don't know. But if I knew I would have the answer.

OK, fine. Can you go back to sleep now?

I think so.

Sleep well then.

Good night.

Sometimes Telemann worries about his children. Heidi plays tennis for seven or eight hours a day and when she's not playing tennis she's thinking about tennis. In much the same way that Telemann thinks about the theatre, Heidi thinks about tennis. The difference is that while there's an element of compulsiveness with Telemann's thoughts about the theatre, a hint of desperation connected with some need to show the buggers what the theatre is capable of, Heidi's thoughts about tennis are completely spontaneous. For instance, she speculates that if she can manage to extend her wrist fully her serve would be more powerful and the ball would be despatched towards her opponent at several more kilometres an hour. And then her mind turns to tennis wear. And equipment. The great thing about Heidi's thinking about tennis, speculates Telemann, is that if she becomes good enough there will be money in it before long. And lots of money at that. Telemann would have no objection to Heidi dethroning Maria Sharapova, the Williams sisters and Jelena Jankovic. He wouldn't at all mind living off Heidi, he has sometimes reflected, with apartments at home and abroad and long hotel stays, in Brazil perhaps, or Dubai, with a free bar and unlimited opportunity to think about the theatre.

Highly unlikely there would be any money in Berthold, though. He's a singularly withdrawn eight-year-old who lives in his own world and is not bothered that others cannot get through to him. Many years after most children have stopped saying strange, charming things Berthold continues to do so. Nina and Telemann exchange glances, sometimes several times a day, and Telemann wonders whether they will ever be able to turn him into a dynamic, viable individual. Sabine is younger and for the time being it is

WE'RE VERY DIFFERENT, YOU and I.

What makes you say that?

I don't know. Perhaps because we're on holiday. Your brain takes charge and goes its own way. Isn't it the same for you?

No.

But we're different.

We are indeed.

You, for example, wear very thick glasses while I don't wear glasses at all.

Mhm.

You use an electric toothbrush. I use a normal toothbrush.

That's true.

You love anything German while I hate it. OK, maybe I don't hate it but I certainly don't love it. I'm sceptical. Sceptical's the word.

Thank you, I get the message. And you take oxidants the whole time while I'm more a fan of anti-oxidants.

I think that's because you're a bit of a shallow person who thinks a lot about appearance and life expectancy and not much about things that really matter.

And what may they be?

I could mention quite a few.

The theatre?

Absolutely. That's one. I will not deny that I consider the theatre to be one of the things that matter.

Do you wish me to think about the theatre as well?

Not at all. Yes, actually I do. Sometimes. Then we could talk. Have more of a meeting of the minds.

After this short conversation Telemann goes out for a smoke. He could have smoked indoors, but he feels sure that Nina would have something to say if he did, and he doesn't want the bother. The whole point of having a fag is to get a few minutes on your own without having to explain or justify yourself, without using any words at all, and while he's smoking he strolls around Mixing Part Churches and passes a sausage stand and orders and thereafter eats a big, big sausage, the largest he can find, full of oxidants, which immediately mount an attack on Telemann's innards. But Telemann loves attacks. Attack is what it's all about. Theatre is synonymous with attack. The mission of the theatre is to break down preconceptions. Above all else, to break down preconceptions. Telemann thinks.

TELEMANN IS LYING ON the sofa and doesn't think much of the YouTube clip entitled Nigella Goes Shopping. She buys Italian-striped ribbons to tie around serviettes for the evening's guests, to whom she will serve Calabrian lamb chops or whatever. He tries to work out why he reacts negatively to this. It worries him. Is he at the turning point in his relationship with Nigella? Is he going to lose her? In which case all he has left is the theatre, he muses.

It could be that her being outside the home is what he finds disturbing. Nigella should be in the kitchen, Telemann believes, but he pulls up short, he doesn't believe that a woman's place is in the kitchen, he has never believed that, but something is wrong because he gets agitated at seeing her in a bric-a-brac shop. This is not Nigella as he knows her. It's a different Nigella. Outside, he can hear Nina laughing and playing with Berthold and Sabine, some summer-type game, which no doubt involves rolling in the grass, the Nazi grass, Telemann thinks. Nazi grass! Christ. That's theatre. He will have to make a note of it. Jumps up and writes something on a random newspaper lying about. NAZI GRASS! In capitals with an exclamation mark. But he has second thoughts, crosses out the exclamation mark. It looks stupid with the exclamation mark. Then it isn't theatre. Just stupid.

Telemann poured himself a glass of wine a short time ago while Nina and the kids were shopping and now he closes his eyes. Laughter from the garden. The usual screech of Bavarian yodelling in the background. The heat. He dozes off. And in the grey area between dozing and being awake he sees something, what's that, he thinks, is it theatre, he hopes it is, it's the perfect situation, he visualises how he will be able to tell journalists and theatre bosses for years to come how he was dozing in Mixing Part Churches when the idea for the monumental, pioneering play just came to him, because he was ready for it, because it was his turn, so to speak.

But it turns out that it isn't theatre. Telemann is slightly unsure what it is. It appears to be some kind of fantasy and Telemann is under the clear impression that it is going to be beneath his dignity, but he can't stop himself, it is insistent. He's in London and spills tea down his trousers in a café and scalds himself and feels a fool and a woman at the next table feels sorry for him and invites him to go with her, she lives just round the corner, and they enter a blue London door and go up a great long staircase and into a gigantic apartment and the woman asks Telemann to take off his trousers so that she can wash and dry them, and he takes off his trousers and she asks if he is hungry and he answers that he is, and she says she is quite good at singing and playing music but sadly bad at cooking, but she has a girlfriend who is really good at it, and she phones her girlfriend, and while she is talking on the phone Telemann notices that the house belongs to the one and only Kate Bush, but not the Kate Bush as she is today, this is Kate Bush as she was at the beginning of the Eighties, but he doesn't mention the fact that he knows who she is, it is as if he instinctively knows that that will ruin the situation, so he keeps his trap shut, and Kate sits down at the piano and says she would like his opinion on a song she has just written, and then she sings *Suspended in Gaffa*, occasionally eyeing him, when the piano allows, with a glance Telemann thinks can only be one of great anticipation, and when the song draws to a close and Telemann gesticulates to say how fantastic the song was, Nigella surges through the door, carrying some cooking ingredients in bags and wearing that very thin turquoise blouse that Telemann is so fond of, and Kate explains the situation to Nigella, who immediately begins to whip cream for some quick comfort eating, but then she spills wine on her blouse and Kate wants to take it off to wash it, but Nigella doesn't think it's necessary, but Kate insists, and in the kerfuffle that ensues when the blouse has to come off, it so happens that some cream gets onto Kate's clothes, so they have to come off too, and after some hesitation while the two women measure each another up, feeling conflicting emotions, they tear each other's clothes

You're not normally so difficult to persuade.

There are so many impressions to deal with at once. A little confusing.

What were you dreaming about?

I don't remember.

Was it about me?

I think ... maybe it was.

Yes, because it wasn't about the theatre, was it.

No. This wasn't theatre, I think. Even though it is not unknown for thinking about the theatre to give me erections

Was it a fantasy ... about me?

The images are a bit vague but ... yes, you could say that.

How exciting. But you don't feel like ...

Maybe not just at the moment.

We'll have to save it for later then.

Yes. We can save that for another day.

JEWISH CUISINE? GOODNESS, WHAT an original birthday present. Thank you very much.

I think you should take a closer look at the title, Telemann.

The Jews have probably got loads of food traditions I know nothing about, that probably Nigella knows nothing about.

Read the title, Telemann.

The … Jewish Question. A History of Anti-Semitism from Olden Times to the Present Day.

Are you giving me a book about anti-Semitism?

I thought you would like it.

Right. Sure. I was just warming to the idea that this was some great tome about Jewish food, so I had to go through a readjustment phase. After all, food is much more pleasant than anti-Semitism.

So you're a little disappointed?

A little. But I'm sure I'll get used to it eventually. Thank you very, very much.

You're welcome. Aren't I going to get a hug then?

Yes.

Many happy returns.

Thanks.

And then, unless I'm much mistaken, the children have some presents for you.

Did they make them themselves, do you think?

Yes.

OK.

This incident makes Telemann nervous. He's afraid Nina has seen through his relationship with Nigella and realised he hates Charles Saatchi. Is the birthday present a subtle hint? It's difficult to imagine that Nina could be so perspicacious, but who knows? We don't really know anyone very well when it comes to the crunch. You can live with people for years without actually knowing what goes on inside their heads. It might transpire that they are living a parallel life to the one they apparently share with you. Some people even have children with their own child. Behind secret doors in the cellar. But they don't show it. Here you have to make a sharp distinction between people and politics whatever the circumstances, Telemann thinks. It's not Jews as such he has problems with. Just Charles Saatchi. Nor has he got any problems with Israel as a nation. God forbid, he doesn't want to be encumbered with any of that. Telemann loves Israel, he thinks. Well, that may be a bit of an exaggeration. But giving anti-Semitism as a birthday present, that's weird. Telemann reckons.

DO WE HAVE TO listen to this Teutonic music?

Define 'have to'.

We seem to be listening to it every night.

Don't you like it?

Nah. There's so much longing in it. It gets tiresome after a while.

Music is normally about longing.

All this bloody longing.

That's your opinion.

What are they all longing for?

The completely normal things that people long for.

Such as?

Well, love, friends, family.

Theatre?

No, I don't think they are longing for the theatre.

I think they are.

OK.

I think that very often when people are longing for other things they are really longing for the theatre.

Do you now?

Yes.

In a way you've formulated your own theory which states that whenever people long for things they are actually longing for the theatre.

Yes.

OK.

They're longing to sit in a dark auditorium with others to be told a story by living people that enables them to see themselves in a new light.

OK.

All this music and yoga and jogging … it's just rubbish.

Yes.

It's theatre they need.

OK.

Aren't you coming with us, Telemann?

I'd rather do some writing.

It would do you good to see the mountains and fill your lungs with fresh air and re-charge your batteries. And your play won't go anywhere.

That's just the problem. I have to get to grips with it.

Come on.

The Baders are coming, too.

For crying out loud.

Nina and Berthold and Sabine want to take the cable car to the top of Zugspitze with the Baders.

Telemann sits down to reflect on the theatre. He thinks about the theatre for five minutes, ten minutes, he thinks about the theatre for fifteen wonderful minutes. Then Heidi wants him to go to tennis practice with her.

I don't know about that. I was thinking of doing a spot of work.

But you never come to the training.

That's not quite true.

When was the last time you came then?

It was … well, it was some time last winter, I suppose.

And what season are we in now?

OK; Jesus Christ, then I'll go with you. But I demand the right to let my mind wander on occasion and to take a few notes.

No worries.

Fine.

Telemann takes a seat in the stands with a pen and a pad he found in the house. He lights a cigarette and closes his eyes, but a groundsman comes and says/tells him that all the court area is a smoke-free zone and has been so for two years. Europe's going to pot, Telemann thinks. And European theatre too.

Telemann watches Heidi playing against a Russian girl. She is good. The Russian, that is. Telemann reflects that in Russia talented youngsters are spotted at three or four years of age and nurtured and nurtured, probably to such an extent that they have no life outside of it. So when at the age of eighteen or twenty they prove not to be the best in the world after all, their lives are in ruins. Heidi is from a different culture and can fall back on a number of things. If all goes well. A couple of things anyway. But having something to fall back on is cowardly nonetheless, Telemann reflects. If you don't have anything to fall back on you become rampant, ruthless, dangerous. That's what people should aim at. In both tennis and in the theatre. Telemann is approaching that good state where the brain takes off and ideas are born. He can feel it. He takes his pen from his pocket and wants to jot down some notes about Russia and groundsmen and risk-taking, this is theatre, all this is potential theatre, but at the top of the pad, in block letters, in an irritating light blue colour, he sees an idiotic logo: HAPPY TIME. That's no bloody good. You can't write theatre on a page that says HAPPY TIME. Typical of the Baders to have a pad like this lying about in the house they rent out. In the thickest swathe of Nazism and incest, there is this atrocious predilection for schmaltz. This region has the world's worst ornaments. Telemann feels sick to the stomach and takes a deep breath to regain some kind of equilibrium. He feels an urge to jot this down, too. About the knick-knacks. The fact that the ornaments must have been here before Nazism. Thus ornaments are dangerous. But he must have another pad. He shouts down to Heidi, who becomes distracted and loses a point.

I need another pad!

What?

I have to get another pad. Can't write on this!

OK.

Telemann leaves the courts and walks toward the town centre smoking. He flings the HAPPY TIME pad, demonstratively and provocatively, to the ground. Several passers-by are taken aback and eye one another and think we don't want this kind of behaviour going on round here.

A woman picks up the pad. She is pleasantly surprised to find it is a pristine writing pad. And moreover HAPPY TIME was written on every sheet. Perfect. She thinks. For correspondence. Fancy throwing this away. Heavens above.

Telemann discovers a book shop and sees a classic notebook. A handy size with rounded corners. An elastic band to keep it closed during transport. A whole host of artists and writers have used the same type according to a poster in the shop. Apollinaire, Picasso, Gertrude Stein, Hemingway and many others. Well, these people did not primarily write plays, Telemann thinks. They mostly scribbled down bits and bobs, and some of them did drawings. Presumably they didn't have it in them to write plays. Anyone can draw, even children. And turning out droll tales is no big deal either, not to mention writing poems, Jeez! Telemann has to laugh. No, theatre is something very different. It's not for your average Joe. But the notebook will have to do. At least there's nothing in blue letters on every page. In fact, they are completely blank. Not even lines. That's good. Lines are not theatre. Empty, blank pages are theatre. A void. A scream in the void. A scream from the bowels of the earth: Angst! Angst! Now that's what Telemann calls theatre.

Back in the stand Telemann writes several things in his new notebook. Russia, he writes, ringing the word, he continues with ruthlessness, smoking laws, Nazi ornaments, maybe he could have a groundsman as a protagonist, why not, they wear smart clothes, they have a job that easily lends itself to symbolism, such as clearing up, repairing what has been destroyed. REPAIRING, Telemann writes, in capital letters underlining the word and allowing the line to continue and become an arrow pointing to another word he hasn't written yet, what could that be now, CLIMATE? He writes CLIMATE, but has second thoughts, climate is boring, it is fundamentally boring, he crosses out the L and turns it into an H, scrubs the final two letters, changes the M to an N, and ends up with CHINA. Repair China? Is that theatre? Telemann spends a long time pondering. Then he smiles. It certainly is.

A woman is sitting a few metres away from him in the stands. Telemann thinks she must be Heidi's opponent's mother. He thinks this because the woman watches the Russian tennis player all the time, and once in a while she lets out small cries and gesticulates with irritation. Actually she might equally well have been her coach, but she doesn't look like how Russian tennis coaches look, in Telemann's view. She's in her thirties and dressed a little bit like an American First Lady. Skirt with matching jacket, that's perhaps what they call a suit, Telemann thinks. Suits are in a way theatre. He makes a note of the word SUIT. The woman is attractive. No two ways about it. He looks at her and she notices him looking.

What are you writing?
    Oh, nothing, really.

It must be something.

Yes. Well, sometimes I hope it will be theatre.

Wow. So you're a theatre writer? A what's it called now
… a dramatist?

That's a big word.

When we're in Moscow we see a lot of theatre.

Oh yes?

A lot.

So your daughter is interested in other things than
tennis, if it is your daughter, that is.

She is my daughter, yes, Anastasia.

Like the Tsar's daughter.

I beg your pardon?

Your daughter's name is the same as the youngest
daughter of the Tsar that was … you know … with his
family … in 1918?

Yes.

I'm sorry.

You're sorry?

That they were killed so brutally, you know, even though
something had to change … well … anyway. She's a good
tennis player.

Your daughter's good, too.

Not as good as yours. But she's OK.

She's not angry enough. But I like her style.

Thank you. So your daughter's angry?

Oh, yes, she's angry alright.

How do you keep her angry?

I have my methods.

I see. And your husband?

What do you mean?

What I mean? … Is he a tennis player too? Is he in Mixing Part Churches?

Mixing Part Churches?

Oh, that's what I call this place.

Right.

So, is your husband here?

No, no. Working.

So, he's a working man?

Absolutely.

Is he … let me guess … something to do with oil? Gazprom? Is he an oligarch?

No, he's not.

Uhuh.

And your wife?

Gone to Zugspitze.

OK.

So you see a lot of theatre?

My husband loves the theatre, Anastasia loves the theatre, I love the theatre.

Fantastic. What kind of theatre do you like?

Chekhov, Mayakovsky, Bulgakov, Shakespeare, but also modern stuff like Harold Pinter and Sarah Kane. We like everything. Do you know Sarah Kane?

Do I know Sarah Kane? Ha! Don't make me laugh. Do you mind if I laugh?

Not at all.

Ha! Ha! Ha! Do I know Sarah Kane? I not only know her, I love her. She is pure theatre. I love Sarah Kane more than myself!

Really?

Yes.

You love her more than yourself?

Well … No … I got carried away. It was … I don't know. I just felt like saying it. But I like her a lot.

I understand.

Thank you.

I think our daughters have finished now.

OK.

So maybe we'll see each other some other time.

Yes. My name's Telemann.

I'm Yelena.

How was Zugspitze?

Unbelievable. We saw the highest point in Germany.

OK.

And we could see deep into Austria, too.

Did you now? Did you see any massed military march past?

Oh, please.

Did you buy any Nazi bric-a-brac?

I don't think that's amusing, Telemann.

You're right.

What about you?

What do you mean what about me?

Did you put pen to paper?

I made a note of four or five words.

Good.

No, it wasn't good.

OK.

Do you know who Sarah Kane is?

What?

I asked you whether you knew who Sarah Kane is.

I don't think so. Ought I to?

Let's keep the 'ought's' out of this. I'm only asking you if you know who she is or not.

I don't know who she is.

OK.

Who is she?

Someone who wrote a handful of brutally truthful plays before she hanged herself at the age of twenty-eight.

My word.

Yes, amazing, isn't it.

Goodness.

An hour later:

Why did you ask me whether I knew who that theatre person was?

I was just wondering.

I don't think you were wondering in an acceptable way.

Maybe not.

You weren't being curious.

Wasn't I?

No. It was more a kind of test.

That wasn't my intention.

Oh yes, it was. You were testing me.

No, I wasn't.

You were trying to find out whether I was up to scratch.

I was just wondering, for Christ's sake!

You were testing me.

Look here: I was thinking about her because I happened to be talking to someone earlier today and then I got curious as to whether you knew who she was, because if so we could maybe talk about her here too, together, you and I, in a way. I like talking about Sarah Kane. I've always known that. That it did me good.

Who were you talking to?

A Russian tennis mummy.

And she knew who this depressive theatre person was?

Yes.

Was she good-looking?

I don't know.

You don't know?

I've never seen her.

But you just said that you were talking to her.

Oh, you mean the Russian?

Of course.

Was *she* good-looking, you mean?

Yes.

I didn't really notice.

Rubbish. Was she good-looking?

Yes.

YOU NEVER PLAY WITH me, Daddy.

Berthold, that's not true.

Yes, it is.

No, it isn't.

You're always thinking about the theatre.

No, I'm not.

You are.

I admit that I think about the theatre a lot. I like theatre.

But you should like me more.

I like you, too. And we did play football today.

Only a few minutes, and anyway I don't like football that much.

You don't like football?

No.

But you should have told me.

I'm telling you now.

OK, then we'll find something else to do. That suits me fine because I don't like football, either.

Then you should have told me.

I'm telling you now. Just like you. But I really thought you loved football.

And that's why you pretended you liked it, too.

I wouldn't put it that way. It's quite normal for parents to encourage their kids in whatever they like doing.

But I don't like football, I said.

No, I thought you did.

Well, now you know.

Yes. OK. So we'll find something else to amuse ourselves with. Any suggestions?

No. You decide.

OK. What shall we do now? Nope, I can't think of anything. Oh, just a moment, what about writing a play together, you and I, from a child's point of view?

No.

Don't say no. We can have a go and if it's boring we can find something else. That's how you find out what you like and who you are.

No.

Don't say no.

LISTEN TO THIS, TELEMANN.

I'm all ears.

Sit down.

You want me to sit down?

Yes.

OK.

Über allen Gipfeln ist Ruh, in allen Wipfeln spürest du kaum einen Hauch …

What does that mean?

It doesn't matter much what it means.

It doesn't matter?

Just listen now.

But what is it?

It's Goethe.

Oh, yes.

Bader gave it to me.

Did he give you a poem?

Yes.

Crikey.

Listen.

OK.

Über allen Gipfeln ist Ruh, in allen Wipfeln …

You've just read that.

You've got to hear it all together.

OK.

Über allen Gipfeln ist Ruh, in allen Wipfeln spürest du kaum einen Hauch. Die Vögelein schweigen im Walde, warte nur, balde, ruhest du auch … Beautiful, isn't it?

Yeah. Yeah. Great. Nice sound. But it's a bit off-putting that I don't understand what it means.

You shouldn't be so focussed on what things mean.

Shouldn't I?

No. The meaning is the most banal aspect of a text, Telemann.

Who says so?

I say so.

Oh yeah.

And Bader.

Does he say so, too?

Yes.

OK, but what does it mean?

It means that darkness has fallen over the mountains and there is peace everywhere. The birds are no longer singing, and in a while you too will be asleep.

Me?

Not you in particular, or, yes, you too, in a way. Whoever's reading the poem. Or listening to it.

So that's me.

Yes.

That I'll be asleep soon, me, too?

Yes.

OK.

What do you think?

It sounds good.

It's more than good, Telemann.

I suppose so.

I would even go so far as to assert that this is the reason why I love Germany.

Would you go that far?

Yes.

Right.

I want you to understand how good this is. Are you capable of sharing my passion?

Perhaps I wouldn't go quite that far.

Some of the way though?

Yes.

But you're still a bit sceptical?

A tiny bit.

Why?

Errr, Goethe was probably quite a fella, and it's beautiful and it's sonorous and rhythmic and all that, but did it stop them becoming Nazis, eh, Nina? And is it theatre? That's what I keep asking myself. When you get down to the nitty gritty, is it theatre?

Nina, I've been thinking.

What about?

You read German and you speak German …

Yes?

But you don't write German.

Well, I do, a bit.

But you don't like to.

That's true.

Why don't you?

I don't know.

Is it something to do with self-confidence?

Could be.

In which case is there something deeper underlying this?

And what might that be?

Could it be that you're basically an insecure person?

I don't think so.

Do you consider yourself self-confident?

Yes, fairly.

I notice you are always shilly-shallying

That's not how I see it.

There, you did it again.

Did I?

You shilly-shallied.

No, I didn't.

Yes, you did, and that makes me begin to wonder if that's what attracts you to all this German stuff.

Eh?

You're insecure. Germany's insecure. And that's why you appeal to each other.

Honestly, Telemann!

Germany's been cowed. It's had to take being held in contempt. It's had to walk around with its back broken for more than sixty years. And you've had it a bit like that inside yourself.

Now, please, give me a break.

You should go to the theatre more.

You what?

Insecure people can learn a lot by going to the theatre.

What?

Germany should go to the theatre, too.

I mean, I ask you.

You should go to the theatre, both of you.

NINA, I'VE BEGUN TO make a list of the people we know who've had cancer. Do you want to see?

Could do.

I've divided them into three columns.

OK.

Those who have died, those who have survived and those where it remains to be seen whether they pull through or not.

I see.

It's not a simple task, if that's what you're thinking.

That's not what I'm thinking.

First of all, it's emotionally challenging, and secondly it's not so easy to remember all of them. The whole lot of them seem to have had cancer.

Mhm. A lot have anyway.

All of them.

No, Telemann, not all of them.

Cancer is theatre, too.

Is it?

Oh, yes, too true. There's not much that is more akin to theatre than cancer.

In other words, it means a lot to you to make lists of this kind.

It's extremely important, Nina. And it's high time, too. It can't wait.

I GOT ON REALLY well with the Baders on the trip to Zugspitze.

Oh, yes. With both of them?

Yes, actually. But maybe especially well with him.

OK.

He's a teacher.

Same as you?

Yes.

How nice.

And he thinks I'm good at German.

I do, too.

He said that at first he thought I came from somewhere around Berlin. He would never have guessed I was Norwegian. He said.

He said that, did he?

And he's coming for lunch today.

Today?

I forgot to tell you.

OK. No problem. I'll sort something out.

Great. But I don't think you should talk about the war.

What? Not even the attempted assassination on Hitler?

No.

But that was the resistance movement who did that?

I don't want that. And nothing at all about the Nazis.

Oh.

Nothing about what happened between 1939 and 1945, anywhere in the world.

What about the First World War?

No.

German unification and the formation of the German Reich in 1871?

No.

The Berlin Wall?

I think not.

But you don't want me to be completely silent, do you?

No.

Can I talk about the theatre?

Preferably not.

Food?

Food's fine. And I think you should tell them something, a story maybe, preferably something funny that doesn't offend any nationality or any individual, and it would be an advantage if it was new to me.

TELEMANN TRAWLS THE TOWN in search of orange blossom water. The Lidl in Olympiastrasse hasn't got it. He looks for some immigrant shops, but it's difficult to find one. Who the hell would emigrate to Mixing Part Churches? In the end, however, he finds a Turkish grocery and his orange blossom water. He is going to make some Arab pancakes with orange blossom syrup. That will give the Baders something to think about, he reckons. They will be expecting pork knuckle and sauerkraut, or maybe something so ur-Norwegian as boiled cod, but they will be getting Arab pancakes with orange blossom syrup. Telemann has to smile. And for dessert it is going to be caramelised pineapple with hot chocolate sauce. Nigella, all of it. Incidentally, it is several days since he has thought about her. The daydream about Nigella and Kate Bush was a heady mix. There has been a lot to process. Just accepting that he is so primitive has come at a cost. I've never seen myself that way, Telemann reflects. I think I'm like so, but if I give free rein to my feelings it is quite clear I am quite a different person. I've never come face to face with myself. That's why I never get going with my theatre work. Not knowing myself is an obstacle. Honesty is the word that suddenly comes to Telemann's mind. In every respect. If I am primitive I have to dare to be primitive lock, stock and barrel. If anyone gets hurt they will have to get hurt. Dishonest theatre is poor theatre. Telemann stops at this point. The bag with the orange blossom water is dangling limply from his clenched fist. He has been struck by a great truth, he believes, in the main street of Mixing Part Churches, slap, bang in the middle of the morning. Honesty is always the best policy. He has to be a hundred per cent honest. To Nina, to the kids, to the Baders and to himself. It is myself I have never met, Sarah Kane once wrote, Telemann remembers. And now he is thinking on those lines himself. He is thinking like a theatre person. Theatre thoughts. At last. Bloody hell. This is going to be theatre.

WHAT DID HE SAY?

Herr Bader says that the caramelised pineapples are very good and he was wondering if he might be so bold as to take one more.

Help yourself.

What did you say just now?

I'm just saying to the Baders that you're going to tell us a story and that I'm a bit curious because I haven't heard it before.

Hm. It's nothing much. It's just something that happened to me in April. An accident.

An accident?

Yes, a minor one.

And you haven't told me about it?

No.

Why not?

I think I repressed the whole incident.

But now you've remembered it?

Yes.

OK. Fire away.

Will you translate as I talk or shall I stop now and then?

I'll translate as you talk.

OK. It happened when you were at a seminar. I can't quite remember where you were …

I was at Voksenåsen.

Voksenåsen?

Yes, that place up in Holmenkollåsen that Norway ceded to Sweden after the war.

I thought we weren't going to talk about the war.

We're not.

OK. Anyway it happened while you were there.

Alright.

What was that you said?

I was just explaining to them that the story itself hasn't begun yet.

I'm starting now.

Great.

So you were at the seminar and I had taken Heidi to tennis and was on my way to pick up Berthold and Sabine, who were visiting friends, and I was driving towards Skøyen, and I was about to turn off a smaller road onto a bigger one, and a cyclist came up on the right, on the pavement, and there was loads of snow, and it was dark too, and the cyclist braked hard as I approached, not very fast, I have to emphasise that, I was driving extremely slowly and carefully. As usual. The cyclist hit his front brake too hard and went over the handlebars, he did a sort of somersault and landed beside the car with a thump. I sat in the car without moving for several seconds and when I didn't hear any more I slowly drove around the corner and stopped, and then I waited. I must have been a bit shocked, it didn't occur to me to get out of the car and see what had happened. I could see in the rear-view mirror the cyclist had got to his feet and was walking towards me. So I leaned over and rolled down the passenger window. I asked him how he was and he said he thought he was alright. Then he said I had driven over his arm.

You drove over his arm?

Evidently. I could see that his forearm was a little bit flat, but he was moving his fingers as normal, and he was smiling too, even though it might have been a slightly strained smile.

What happened?

I asked whether he wanted me to take him anywhere, but he didn't. So then I wished him a speedy recovery and drove off.

You drove off?

Yeah.

And you didn't give it another thought?

No. But it's been on my mind recently.

So that's why you've been a bit distracted, is it?

I don't think so. But I don't consider that the crash was my fault. He was totally to blame. Where I went wrong was to drive around the corner, not to stop at once, because that's when I must have driven over his arm … What was that he said?

Herr Bader says you shouldn't have driven around the corner.

I just said that. What's he saying now?

He says you should have stopped at once, as soon as the cyclist drove into the car and you should have got out to see what had happened.

Tell Herr Bader that in my opinion he should mind his own business.

I'm not saying that.

Tell him!

No.

What did you say just now?

I said that you said we're grateful that they accepted our invitation and that you and your wife, me that is, thank them for allowing us to rent this wonderful house.

Bloody hell, I can see I'll have to learn German.

Yes, do.

What are they saying now?

They're thanking us for the nice food and the pleasant company and the interesting story you've just told them.

The pleasure was all fucking ours.

It's NOT VERY NICE to think that you keep things hidden from me.

I don't keep things hidden.

You drive over people's arms without telling me. That's … not very nice. It worries me.

I thought it was horrible, so I repressed it. I haven't thought about it since it happened.

And then it suddenly, like, came back to you?

Yes.

Why?

Because you asked me to tell you a story you hadn't heard before. That's quite an ask, but I took your request seriously and that was what I came up with.

Is there anything else?

What do you mean anything else?

Other things you haven't told me?

I don't think so.

You don't think so?

No, I don't think so.

No other accidents, large or small?

No.

You haven't killed anyone?

No.

But you're not absolutely sure?

What do you mean?

If you think it was so horrible to drive over a cyclist's arm it's so much more horrible to take someone's life and then I assume you would have it repressed it all the more.

You're quite right.

But no bells are ringing?

Now I think you're going too far, Nina.

I also think it's strange of you to tell us about driving over a cyclist's arm when we have guests from abroad to dinner. You're not just representing yourself, Telemann, you're an ambassador me as well, and in a way, your country. Now the Baders no doubt think that Norwegians are out of their minds.

Fine. Next time I'll tell a different story.

If there is a next time.

What do you mean?

I don't know.

What are you on about now?

I'm just saying that you make me insecure, Telemann. I'm not sure that you can distinguish between fiction and reality in ways other adults can follow.

Now I have no idea what you mean.

You live in a world where recollection and fantasy sometimes merge, but this is not theatre, Telemann, this is us, it's you and me and our children on holiday and we're trying to talk to other people, but thanks to you it went off the rails, it ended in a scene, and you might know what's in your own head, but those around you have no idea.

Is that a big problem?

Yes, I think it is.

But it did happen. The cyclist actually hit the car and I drove over his arm.

Right.

His arm was a bit flat afterwards.

OK, good night.

Good night.

WHAT ON EARTH ARE you up to?

I'm making breakfast.

It looks more like dinner.

But it's breakfast.

You're going to have dinner for breakfast?

No. I'm having breakfast.

But it looks like dinner.

Now you're beginning to grate, Nina.

What?

You won't like me saying so and I would like you to observe that I am not raising my voice or straining it when I say this, but if an unbiased outsider had been listening to what you just said I would not have blamed them for thinking you were a very conventional and boring person.

Are you saying I'm a boring person?

I feel uncomfortable about having to justify myself in this way. We're on holiday. We have no plans. When I woke up I lay in bed, happily thinking about the theatre, and then I got hungry and now here I am, making Three Fishes with Three-Herb Salsa, because I'm keen to see what it tastes like. What time of the day it might be and the conventions regarding what it is usual to eat for breakfast are of no interest to me.

You don't think it is off-putting that Nigella is in the process of putting food into her mouth in this picture?

No.

So Nigella is not boring?

I don't know.

But what do you think?

I don't think she's boring.

I'm not boring, either.

Of course not.

But you just said I was.

What I said was that you could easily be mistaken for a boring person.

Because I think it's strange to have dinner for breakfast?

Yes.

Whereas you are an interesting person?

I didn't say that.

But I think you believe that.

I may be a little more open than you. A little more boundless. Maybe.

Maybe I don't think there's any point in being boundless.

Perhaps you're right.

Exactly.

Let's leave it like that then.

Yes.

Would you like to try some?

No.
Later?
Maybe.
For dinner?
Possibly.

DID YOU KNOW THAT there are actually two towns?

Er … no.

That's what Bader just told me.

Did he now?

Garmisch was originally one town and Partenkirchen another.

Really?

And then they were merged before the Winter Olympics in 1936.

I see.

But the locals were against it.

OK.

Hitler just decided.

Hitler would.

And today many tourists call the town just Garmisch, but it's unfortunate because that annoys those living in Partenkirchen, according to Bader.

And which bit are we in now?

Partenkirchen.

So Bader is annoyed?

Must be a little.

Did you console him?

At least I spoke with a calm, warm voice.

Good. But as long as we call it Mixing Part Churches we elegantly avoid the whole problem.

I think you should stop saying that.

I will not.

This is about identity and self-respect. You don't mock that.

I do.

What if the Germans called Oslo some stupid name?

They're welcome to. Sometimes I feel like doing the same myself.

I'll have to make a note of that by the way. Have you got any suggestions?

No.

Have you got a pen?

No.

Telemann?

Yes.

Are you aware that whenever you smoke a fag you shorten your life by eleven minutes?

I wasn't, no.

But that's the truth of the matter.

OK.

What do you think when you hear that?

I don't know. Eleven minutes is not the end of the world.

No, but if you add all the cigarettes you've smoked it amounts to months and years.

You can't think like that.

Can't you?

No. A pack of ten makes a hundred and eleven minutes. That corresponds to quite a long film or, for example, one of the short performances we often put on in the Malersal in the National Theatre.

What do you mean?

There are many films and plays that are not worth seeing, so you can say that if I begin to skip the ones I know won't give me anything, and that is most of them, it more or less evens itself out.

Are you being serious?

Of course I am.

Sometimes I wonder if you're all there.

I certainly am. I've got a lot of opinions about you too, but I keep them to myself.

Have you?

Yes.

Such as?

I don't wish to comment.

I think that's cowardly of you.

I don't think you've thought this through well enough, Nina.

I want to know what you think about me.

No comment.

But you love me?

Yes, of course.

ARE YOU ASLEEP?

What?

I was asking if you were asleep.

What do you think?

May I say something?

I suppose so.

I was thinking about what we were saying earlier today.

Mhm?

I think it's important that we say what we think about each other, and that should go for everything, at any time.

You're not afraid of it getting too brutal?

If it does, so be it.

When shall we start then?

Now, right now.

OK. I think, for example, it's a bit irritating to be kept awake like this, just when I was dropping off.

But this is important.

Yes, but there's always tomorrow morning. And nothing's going to happen between us before then anyway.

You mean I should have waited?

Yes.

TURN LEFT.

Sure?

According to the map the castle should be a few kilometres away.

What does that scowl mean?

I'm a tiny bit annoyed.

What about?

I find the way you drive irritating.

Just today or always?

Always.

I don't think it is.

Yes, it is. First, you spend too long in first gear, then you're too long in second, and if the wipers are on and it stops raining you don't turn them off. You simply don't notice that the wipers are churning away for no reason, and not only that, you remove the ignition key far too quickly when you stop. The key gets bent like that.

It doesn't look bent to me.

No.

You're wrong then.

No, I'm not. I straighten the key when you're not looking.

For my sake, you mean.

Yes, or rather, I don't really know why. I just don't want the key to be bent.

It gets on my nerves that you don't know why.

You were the one who wanted us to be frank and open.

You're right.

I thought that was how you wanted things to be.

Yes, but maybe not when the children can hear.

Right. So in other words what I just said was a little bit OK and a little bit not OK.

Yes.

But a good start nonetheless.

Yes. By the way, I think you should start using a tooth-pick.

What?

There's something peculiar about your teeth which causes food to get stuck in the gaps. It's disgusting. I really have to force myself to kiss you. And that's not all.

Bugger me!

Does what I say make you angry?

Yes, it does. We were actually discussing the castle.

True enough. Look, children.

Who on earth built that?

Ludwig the Second. I've told you loads about him.

Yes, you have. What a bloody castle! The fella who had that built was completely bonkers, a mental case, a fruitcake, what's the word for it these days, Heidi? What do you lot say?

We just say mad.

OK, the fella who built this was mad. Nina, would you say it would be correct to assert that there was a link between Ludwig the Second and National Socialism.

No.

Not just an itsy-bitsy, mega-tiny link.

No.

OK. Did you hear that, kids? No link between Ludwig the Second and National Socialism according to your mother. Who wants an ice cream?

HEY, THERE'S THE WOMAN I met in Lidl.

Who?

The American woman I told you about, who had a wedding cake made in the shape of this castle and all that.

Oh yes. Where is she?

Over there, by the wall.

Right.

Do you think I should go over and say hello.

No.

Why not?

I don't know. I just don't think you should.

OK, but now she's coming over here.

Kiss me!

What?

Kiss me.

Of course I'd love to, but why now?

Uh oh, too late.

Hi!

Hello. This is my wife, Nina.

I'm Lisa.

Hello.

Sorry to bother you, but I just wanted to say hello. It's an amazing castle, don't you think?

Yes.

Absolutely. And I like the fact that the king who built it was a raving lunatic.

What?

And a homosexual, although there's nothing wrong with being a homosexual of course.

What?

You didn't know?

I never understand you guys and your humour. But we love it here anyway. We have so much fun in Europe.

Yes, we do, too.

OK. I'll go look for my family now. Take care.

You, too. Goodbye. Shall I kiss you now?

No.

TELEMANN IS LOOKING FOR something to make for dinner and comes across a photograph of Nigella shaking a cocktail mixer with a smile on her face. He feels a pang of something close to longing. Why does Nina never go round smiling and shaking cocktails? It's as if there is no scope in their relationship for such a possibility. What makes this situation especially titillating is that Nigella is wearing a T-shirt with a Playboy bunny logo. The colours in the photo have been treated in a slightly odd way so that it is not easy to get a clear view of the T-shirt, Telemann thinks, but he assumes it is black and that the logo is in silver with a kind of glitter effect. Quite a showy T-shirt, all in all. Especially as Nigella's curves are clearly visible. Did she buy it herself? Telemann thinks. Could Nigella have gone out in London and bought this T-shirt? And did she actively search it out or did she come across it when she was actually looking for something else? These are important questions as aspects of her personality can be deduced from the answers.

What are you thinking about?

Oh, hello. I didn't hear you come in.

No. I didn't make any noise.

I see. I'm just looking for something to make for dinner.

But there aren't any recipes on the page you're looking at.

I haven't got past the thinking stage yet. I'm deliberating.

What about?

Well … nothing special.

Don't you think that's a bit much, wearing a Playboy T-shirt?

What?

Don't pretend you don't know what I'm talking about.

Yes, well, maybe it is a bit much. Yes, it is.

But you quite like it too, don't you.

Listen to me: I was just sitting here with the cookery book open at a random page and then I got carried away, as usual, sort of, it's the theatre again of course, playing games with me. That's all there is to it.

OK. Do you want me to make dinner for once?

If you want to.

What would you prefer?

I'd prefer to make it myself.

You like making dinner?

Yes.

You never used to.

No.

You've changed then?

I must have done.

Good.

Yes, since you've brought the matter up I feel I'm probably going through a more or less constant process of change and evolution. Not only with regard to food but maybe especially as far as food is concerned.

OK.

Are you not undergoing change?

I might well be. It's hard to say.

Yes, it's hard. It's a terribly complicated process. And painful.

Do you think it's painful?

No, not really.

But that's the term you used?

Yes.

What if Charles Saatchi had bought the T-shirt for Nigella?

The thought hits Telemann like a meteor. It's been heading towards him for years, although he hasn't been aware of it. And now it hits him and destroys all life. Cripes! Telemann thinks. Saatchi, the dirty old bugger. He is considered a philanthropist who buys art and makes it available to the general public free of charge and doesn't want his name to be in the limelight. The dirty lecher. Now things are falling into place. Saatchi sees Nigella as his own private toy. By dint of cunning and money and shadowy fame he has lured her into a fiendish trap. And dewy-eyed Nigella fell for it. She obeys his every wish. That explains the photograph in the taxi, too. Saatchi has no need to sit close to her because he owns her, body and soul. He has tamed and bewitched her. The world at large believes she is free. They see her recording cookery programmes and writing books and making appearances all over the place, but in fact she is imprisoned in a sick man's mind.

Suddenly Telemann understands how it all fits. For the first time he sees that Nigella is in danger. She is being exploited in the most ruthless way. She needs help. Jesus Christ. Jesus. Christ.

Telemann?

Er … yes.

Is there something wrong? You're so pale.

I … I feel dizzy.

Have you got a temperature?

I don't know.

Yes, you have. You're hot.

Yes, I feel quite hot.

Do you want me to make dinner after all?

Yes, you could do.

OK.

I think I'll go and have a lie-down.

Yes, do.

Dad?

Be quiet, Berthold! Dad's thinking about the theatre.

But Dad!

Is it important?

Yes.

OK, then, out with it.

Guess what I'm going to be.

Do you mean when you grow up?

Yes.

Hmmm … no, give up.

Guess!

OK … something to do with transport?

No. I'm going to be a lawyer. Or someone with a top job on Oslo City council.

Blimey, alright, have you spoken to Mum about it?

Yes, but what do *you* think?

Both sound good, Berthold. Great stuff.

Do you think I'm up to that?

Well, I don't know. I would be the first to be overjoyed if you succeeded, but in all honesty I think you're too scatty.

What do you think the future holds for me?

Can you bear to hear the truth?

Yes.

I think you're going to end up as a shuttlecock in the social security system.

What's that?

That's a person nobody wants to employ and is sent from department to department until all his resistance is broken down and he's dependent on disability benefit.

OK.

Mum and I will of course help to the best of our ability. We can write letters for you and you're welcome to live at home for a little longer than is normal. We'll sort something out.

OK.

And after you've been bitter for a few years then maybe you can write some drama for the theatre.

Do you think so?

That remains to be seen, but I don't think we should rule it out.

HEY TELEMANN! BADER'S OUTSIDE.

And?

He's wondering whether you want to go walking with him.

What?

That's what he said. He's sorry that our dinner ended up in a bit of a bad atmosphere and he's wondering whether you want to go walking with him so that you can get to know each other better.

What kind of walk?

Probably just the usual type.

Say hello and no.

I think you should say yes.

But I'm saying no.

I think you should say yes.

WHAT DID HE SAY?

He said you should tighten the laces on your boots and then he asked which mountain you'd like to climb.

Makes no difference to me. What's he saying now?

You should have a look. There are mountains everywhere and you can choose the one you like best.

I have no way of judging what's good or bad. What's he saying now?

He says that this mountain here is called Zugspitze, that one there is Alpspitze, and then there's Wank, Eckbauer, Hausberg and Kreuzeck.

Can't you tell him I'd rather stay at home and think about the theatre and work on my list of people who have had cancer?

No.

Can you ask Bader if he knows anyone who has had cancer?

No.

You're a useless interpreter.

I am not.

Interpreters shouldn't select which bits to pass on. They

should be neutral intermediaries. They shouldn't distort the message.

We'll leave that discussion for later.

What's he saying?

He wants to know which mountain.

Right, bloody hell, it'll have to be Zugspitze, at least it's not as high as the others. What's he saying now?

He say he likes to take the cable car up and walk down, but if you prefer to walk up, that's fine with him.

Walk up? Are you mad?

Then I'll tell him his suggestion sounds good to you.

I bet you will.

Have a nice walk!

Thank you very much.

GERMAN, GERMAN, GERMAN, GERMAN, German.

I don't understand a word you're saying, Bader, not a single word, so there's no point in saying anything. Can't we just walk in silence? It's beautiful here, I'll give you that. Actually it's fantastically beautiful.

German, German, German, German.

Can't you just put a sock in it?

German, German, German, German, German, German, German.

What are you going on about now? Is it the war? I bet it's the war.

German, German, German.

Do you mean the First World War? Yes, it was terrible. That fiendish idea of the trenches. All the more surprising that it was you lot who started the Second World War.

German, German.

It was becoming a bit of a habit. You didn't think about anything else but war. That was how it was, wasn't it? You couldn't have enough of it.

German, German, German.

Yes, that's what I think, too.

German, German, German, German.

I agree. Hello, there's a kiosk over there.

German, German.

Are you asking if I want an ice cream? Yes please. Very nice of you.

German, German, German, German.

Don't get me wrong, Bader, I'm not blaming you, I'm sure you're a great fella. And it's high time we put all these wars behind us. Nina says you already have done, and are moving forward, in an impressive manner. And maybe that's right.

German, German.

Indeed, but let's not talk about it any more. Let's talk about the theatre instead. After all German theatre has a pretty good reputation. I don't think you understand what I'm saying.

German, German?

German theatre, yes! Deutsches Theatre!

Jawohl!

And not forgetting the Volksbuehne. Isn't that what it's called? In Berlin? And Fassbinder, he made some films, but in a way films are theatre too, at least on one level, if you get what I mean.

German, German, Fassbinder?

Yes, now we're communicating, Bader. Holy shit!

EXCUSE ME, BUT NOW we've been walking for hours. I want to go home.

German, German.

Isn't there a shortcut? Or perhaps we can catch a bus for the last part of the way?

German, German, German, German, German, German, German, German, German, German, German, German.

Hey, I think you're sounding a little down in the mouth. Chin up, Badermann.

German, German, German.

Are you still going on about the war? I thought we'd put that behind us. Or is it just that you're a bit on the slow side? Or perhaps you love to talk about the war but feel it's difficult because you and your compatriots have been left with the blame and the shame.

German, German.

If you want we can talk about shame.

German, German, German.

No, this is pointless, Bader, we're getting nowhere. I suggest you shut up and we can both think about the things we like best.

German.

OK. I, for my part, am going to think about theatre. And a little about Nigella.

Nigella?

Nigella, yes.

JA! JA! Nigella!

That's the one.

German, German, German.

Calm down, man! Now you're getting vulgar. True, Nigella is fascinatingly voluptuous, but you mustn't forget that behind the façade there is a fragile and lonely heart beating away, caught in the web of a sick Jew. Forget that I said Jew! I shouldn't have said that, it's got nothing to do with the matter and it's particularly bad taste around these parts. Pretend you didn't hear it. But the point remains the same: Nigella consoles all of us with her food. But who consoles her, Bader? Eh? Eh? Who consoles Nigella?

German, German, German.

You're not answering my question.

German, German?

Can you hold my hand? You must be joking.

How was the walk with Bader?

Not bad.

Don't you feel like talking about it?

Not a lot to say. We took the cable car up. We walked down.

Did you chat?

He talked a lot about the war, I think. I tried to follow as best I could.

Did you two have a laugh?

I can't remember us laughing.

Pity.

But he bought me an ice cream.

Did he?

A big one.

Good.

Actually by the end we were beginning to hit it off. It transpired that we shared a common interest.

What was that?

I'm not quite sure. But I think it was food. But it could well have been something else.

Such as?
I don't want to say.
You don't want to say?
No.

NINA!

Yes? What is it?

I just made contact with my reptile brain.

What?

My reptile brain.

Oh yes?

It was quite extraordinary, almost unreal, but at the same time quite real, if you see what I mean, like theatre.

Was it now?

Do you want to hear any more?

If you like.

I was thinking about the theatre, as usual, in fact I was just on the point of making a note about something I thought should be made a note of when I became aware of some movement at the edge of my field of vision.

Go on.

My brain immediately transmitted chemical signals left, right and centre, I don't know what they're called, but I've heard about serotonin and dopamine and adrenalin, so it's conceivable that some of these chemicals were involved in this case, too. I could feel it in my backbone, and in my forehead, a kind of stabbing, hot impulse, and my muscles tensed, I felt I was about to wave an arm, the left one, I think, and also about to panic.

Heavens.

Do you know what the movement I saw was?

No.

It was the end of a tea bag, where there was no tea, the end with the paper tag with Lipton written on it, or in this case: Teekanne Liebesfrucht.

Really.

The paper tag was swaying to and fro beside the cup. My brain must have imagined it was a poisonous spider and was preparing itself to kill it. It was a matter of life and death, you see.

Goodness.

It or me, it was.

How dramatic.

It was, wasn't it? It was theatre at its best. Forgive me for repeating myself. It was just as good as theatre.

Golly.

I need to come to terms with all this, Nina. Do you mind if I go for a little walk on my own?

Not at all.

I'D LIKE A SIDEBOARD.

I see.

With a fern leaf carving on it.

Well, you've just had your birthday.

Yes, I know, but I'm just telling you, so that there's no need to ask next time you're buying me a present.

Fine.

The sideboard should be about this high and the fern leaf shouldn't be too small.

I see.

And I want it on the right of my desk at home, in front of the window.

What made you think of that?

I don't know.

Stop saying that.

What?

Stop saying I don't know.

But what if I don't know?

You know very well. It's just a way of cutting short the conversation so that you can carry on with your own thoughts.

OK.

So what made you think of sideboards and ferns?

I've seen numerous photos of theatre people with fern sideboards. Actors, directors, playwrights.

The whole caboodle had one. Darwin did, too.

Darwin?

Yeah.

I didn't think he had anything to do with the theatre. Depends on the eye of the beholder. The theory of evolution is theatre too, in a way.

And in a way it isn't.

Yes, indeed. You have to keep your mind open.

But you still think that sideboards, ferns and theatre-thoughts go hand in hand.

I think one presupposes the other.

So ferns and sideboards cannot be separated from theatre-thoughts?

And vice versa.

Vice versa?

That's the way it is. It all suddenly seems so obvious. Fancy my never seeing the connection before now. Crazy.

But it's quite a radical idea.

Quite possibly.

So you consider yourself a radical?

That could be the case. But I can't wait for my next birthday.

Can you not?

Every minute theatre-thoughts in my head are going to waste.

That must be absolutely intolerable.

Yes, I'm glad you understand me. Would you have any objection to my acquiring a sideboard with ferns at my own expense?

Not at all.

Do you think there are any here in Mixing Part Churches?

It's not called Mixing Part Churches.

TELEMANN!

Hm?

You're talking in your sleep.

What?

You're keeping me awake.

Was I talking?

Yes.

What did I say?

What do you think?

I don't know.

Stop saying you don't know.

I don't know what I said. As I was asleep.

You were talking about another woman.

Was I?

Yes.

Which one?

You didn't say. But you were going to save her. You said you were going to save her.

Did I say that?

Yes.

It was you.

No, it wasn't.

Yes, it was. Surely I would know best what I was dreaming.

Were you going to save me?

Yes, someone had kidnapped you.

Who?

The Germans.

Which Germans?

I think it was theatre people. I didn't like them. And then they kidnapped you. And then I saved you.

Crikey. How heroic of you.

It was the least I could do.

Shall we get a few more hours' sleep?

Yes, let's.

After this Telemann lies awake. He feels it was a close shave. He can't go on like this. Should he suggest that Nina and he have separate rooms? In which case it would have to be well planned so that she doesn't take it amiss. He will have to put the blame on theatre. Beset by his thoughts, day and night, he has to be able to switch on the light and take notes, write, not to mention being able to talk out loud to himself, or laugh, maybe even cry, at any time. And he doesn't want to be disturbed. He's never been the type to enjoy disturbing others. Nina knows that. And she knows that he's helped other playwrights for years. Saved their bacon even. Without ever asking to be credited. He's hidden his light under a bushel. In a word. He has had enough of that. He was going to write the pants off them. Too bloody true. They think they can write plays, but the stuff he was going to write … Lord-a-mercy.

Telemann rests his fists on his chest and thrusts them into the air. He does it several times and says Ah! He says AH! He says Theatre. He says THEATRE! He says AH! THEATRE! And he says Sod'em! Sod'em! THEATRE! AH!

What do you think you're doing?
    Nothing.
    Lying there and punching the air?
    Not any more.
    But that's what you were doing?
    Yes.
    Should I be worried?
    I don't think so.
    You're still the same person?
    More or less.
    What was that you were saying as you punched the air?
    Nothing.
    Don't say nothing. I heard you saying something.
    It was nothing important.
    I think it was important.
    I said theatre.
    Theatre?
    Yes.

You really like the theatre, Telemann, don't you.

Yes, I do.

You love the theatre.

Yes.

When are you going to start writing?

Very soon.

NINA, SOMETHING'S JUST OCCURRED to me.

Yes?

We haven't made love for some time

Haven't we?

No.

Right.

In my opinion, if this were a really good holiday we would have already done it a few times.

So you don't think it's a good holiday?

No, no, I do.

But not really good?

No.

How many times would we have had to do it?

A couple of dozen.

That many?

Actually, yes.

I think the holiday is fine as it is.

Yes, it is fine. But if were to be mega-fine.

You have to be careful not to place excessive demands on life.

I don't think that's an excessive demand.

It's easy to be disappointed if you make too many demands.

I don't make so many demands.

You'll have to learn to love things closer to home, Telemann.

For me, being in bed with you is being close to home.

Rubbish.

WHAT ABOUT DOING IT NOW?

Doing what?

What we've just been talking about.

Were we talking about something?

Yes.

Oh, that. That's not a good idea.

Yes, it is.

No, it isn't.

Yes, it is.

I don't think it is.

Why not?

Telemann … I don't like to have to say this, but …

But what?

I think I'm becoming allergic.

Allergic?

Yes.

To what?

To you.

What?

I'm afraid I'm developing a kind of allergy to you.

What do you mean?

Last week when you stroked me a bit before we fell asleep I got a rash right down the back of my thigh, and in the last few days my skin has become irritated where you touched me. Here, for instance, where you put your hand last night, here on my arm, when you said you thought my glasses were nice despite the lenses being quite thick, and touched my arm, in a way as if to emphasise the friendly nature of what you said.

Oh?

It's irritated all over. Can you see?

This is madness, Nina.

Madness to some maybe. These things happen, it's the way of the world.

Don't you like me any more?

It's not a question of liking or not liking. My body is trying to tell me something.

And you're listening?

My body knows.

Are you sure of that?

Oh, yes, Telemann. The body knows. Yours does too.

Mine's trying to tell me we should make love a couple of dozen times.

That's of no interest to my body.

So what it's trying to tell you then?

I don't know.

But it doesn't sound too promising for our relationship, to say the least.

No, agreed.

Maybe it's because I didn't wash my hands carefully enough after cooking. Nigella uses lots of spices which are sometimes rather exotic. Maybe your skin reacts to external contact with them.

It's not that, Telemann, it's you.

How can you be sure of that?

I just can.

No, you can't.

Anyway it's her fault.

Eh?

Nigella's.

Eh?

She's stuffed your head with crazy ideas.

Eh?

It's her fault.

Are you jealous of Nigella?

No. I just don't like her.

Is it because she has big breasts, and is always happy and hungry?

I think you want to be free of me, and Nigella has made your body produce some substance which pushes me away from you.

Eh?

That's what I believe.

There's no way I can get Nigella.

Ha! So that means you do want to have her.

Wanting her can be many things. That's not how life works.

You want to have her!

Of course I want her on one level. But that has nothing to do with the real world. If I hadn't been married to you, but fancy-free and attractive in Nigella's eyes and she had knocked on my door and had offered herself I would not have said no, I have to admit, then I would have gone for it, ho ho, but that is not a scenario that I visualise or have any intention of trying to bring to fruition.

You're kidding yourself.

No, I'm not.

Yes, you are.

Come on, Nina.

Stop saying 'come on'. It's a form of bossiness. It's patronising.

What?

Don't say 'come on'.

I'll say what I like. Nigella lives in Eaton Square in London, in a house worth maybe 70 million. She's one of the world's most famous TV chefs, and on top of that she's married to one of the richest men in Britain. You and I, on the other hand, are here, in southern Germany, in Bavaria, the cradle of Nazism …

Don't say the cradle of Nazism.

I'll bloody well say what I like. If I want to say 'come on', I'll say 'come on'. If I want to say the cradle of Nazism,

I'll say the cradle of Nazism.

I think you should show some respect for what I think you shouldn't say.

Will you let me finish?

Alright.

What I was in the middle of saying was that we, you and I, are fairly ordinary people, you're a teacher and I'm a theatre person ...

You're a theatre director, Telemann, that's what you are.

That's right, but I'm trying to ... yes, well, the point nonetheless is that neither you nor I lives in a dream world, on the contrary we work quite hard, live in a normal house, have three kids and at this moment we're on holiday and when I ask you to make love you give me this crazy tale about irritated skin and Nigella causing me to produce substances that push you away from me. I'm here, Nina! With you! In Mixing Part Churches!

It's not called Mixing Part Churches.

COME ON! DO YOU realise what you're saying?

Don't say 'come on'.

But do you realise what you're saying?

Of course I realise what I'm saying.

This is absolutely insane. I'm not going to leave you, you know that.

Yes, you are. That's what you want. You walk around lost in thought and when I ask you something you always say you're thinking about the theatre.

But that's what I *am* thinking.

No, you're not.

Yes, I am.

Let me see what you've written!

Eh?

Let me see what you've written this holiday!

But ...

No buts!

I haven't written that much.

Let me see!

I think a lot. And then I delve deeper. And then I might make a note of some idea or other and add some more abstract concept. And as I normally work a lot with other people's material, I rarely get a chance to consider my own stuff, but that's what I'm doing here. I'm thinking about the theatre all day long. For example, just before we began this discussion or conversation or whatever you want to call it, what do you reckon I was thinking about?

Theatre?

Spot on. There you go.

I want to see what you've written!

WHAT'S RUSSIA SUPPOSED TO mean?

It's just a note, Nina.

Yes, but why Russia?

What it means?

Yes.

It's hard to talk about.

Try.

It means nothing.

Nothing?

Yes, nothing.

So why did you make a note of it?

I don't know. It's intuition at work.

What's the point of it?

You tell me. Maybe it can be combined with something else and I can make something of it.

In connection with the theatre?

That's the plan.

What do you mean by Nazi bric-a-brac?

Nazi bric-a-brac. Which everyone has round here. Bader's house is full of it.

So, in your opinion, the Baders are Nazis.

No.

But they've got Nazi bric-a-brac?

Yes. Or else … yes, they have.

But for them they're primarily ornaments, don't you think?

Naturally.

So they don't realise they've got Nazi bric-a-brac?

I think they know. In their heart of hearts.

You've written REPAIR in capital letters?

Indeed.

And you've underlined it and there's an arrow pointing to another word. What's that you've got? Climate? China?

China.

So it says REPAIR CHINA?

Yes.

And what's this here?

Suit.

Suit?

Yes.

I think Russia is a code word for Nigella.

Eh?

The same number of letters.

Now you're really stretching it, Nina.

Don't try and talk your way out of this. Russia and Nigella have the same number of letters. Explain that to me. Now I'm really curious.

There aren't the same number of letters. Russia's got six

and Nigella's got seven.

One two three four five six. One two three four five six seven. OK.

Do you think I really need to encode Nigella's name?

Yes, I do. So Russia isn't a code word then?

Come on now. I don't write in code.

Don't say 'come on'.

So THIS IS HOW much you've done in two weeks?

By and large. But all you can see is the tip of the iceberg. Beneath the surface there is cubic kilometre upon cubic kilometre of thought, invisible to the naked eye.

Bit thin, that one, Telemann.

It's theatre.

I think it's thin.

You don't know what you're talking about. This is the quintessence of theatre. This is the stuff of which theatre is made.

It's nothing, Telemann. It's nothing.

It's theatre.

No.

The truth is, Nina, that you have no conception of what theatre is. You would not recognise theatre if people danced naked in front of you yelling at you through megaphones that this was theatre.

I'm allergic to you, Telemann.

You don't know what theatre is.

I'm allergic. Look! I come out in a rash when you talk.

You don't know what theatre is.

I'm allergic to theatre.

Dad?

Mhm?

If we'd been elephants, we would have been five elephants.

Yes.

Crazy thought?

Yes, it is actually.

Imagine that!

Yes, good thinking, Berthold. Great.

BADER ONLY EATS EGGS from hens that can see snow-capped mountains.

I see.

Schneeberg eggs.

Does he now.

Don't you think that's nice?

Yes, I do.

Charming even?

Absolutely. Shall we make love?

Not now.

Some other time?

Alright.

ARE YOU COMING WITH us to Zugspitze?

What, again?

Yes, Heidi's been a bit upset because we didn't take her along last time, so now all three of us are going. And Bader too, by the way.

Bader, too?

Yes.

I'll stay here then.

OK.

I'll stay here, have a smoke and think about the theatre.

Alright.

As soon as Nina and the kids are out of the house it is Telemann-time.

With some red wine and a notebook in his hand, he locks himself in the toilet and thinks about the theatre. Nina's toothbrush whirrs away in the background. Notes have to be made. Bugger her. Nina would soon see who can make notes. How dare she comment on his notes in the first place! And what they mean. And how few of them there are. Ridiculous. What a cheek. What. A. Cheek.

Telemann! Are you in there?!

What?!

Open up!

I thought you'd gone!

We had gone, but Berthold needs to go to the loo!

Right!

Are you going to open the door?

No.

Why not?!

Because I'm on the loo!

Have you nearly finished then?

No.

What's that sound I can hear?

Nothing.

What did you mean, nothing?!

There's nothing making any noise in here!

Yes, there is!

No, there isn't!

Is it my toothbrush?

No!

It must be. Let me in!

No!

Let me in!

The sound's in your mind, Nina!

What?!

It's the allergy playing you up. It's all in your mind.

Berthold needs the loo.

Find another loo!

What did you say?!

I said find another loo!

Jesus Christ. Not even in the loo is Telemann-time respected. What's this country coming to? Telemann thinks. What. Is. This. Country. Coming. To. He notes down the words, looks at them and can see they are good. There's no doubt. He's getting close to something approximating theatre. But what does that really mean? Because when he says country he doesn't mean Germany, of course. Nor Norway. He means the family, no, the situation, or maybe even the state he is now. And the state the theatre is in now. And the state of the theatre in him now. The theatre in him. That's getting closer. Where is this country going to? Could that be a title? Have we got a title here? Telemann clasps the notebook with shaking hands. This is real theatre. A country which isn't a country but a cross between a state and a person. There can hardly be any doubt that this is theatre. Nothing less.

Well, Berthold's wet his pants!

What?!

I'd just like to inform you that Berthold peed himself just as he was going into Bader's toilet! So thank you very much!

OK! My pleasure! Have a nice walk!

Wonderful. Is it any wonder that the theatre is stagnating and having a hard time? In conditions like these it's amazing that there is any decent theatre at all. But then it's not supposed to be easy. Theatre has to be painful. That's its primary function, to be painful. It has to be painful for the creator, the mediator and, not least, the receiver. If any element fails to be painful, it's not theatre. Then it's no more than a simple performance. Did it hurt? That should be the criterion for everyone leaving the theatre. The theatre should, as a matter of rule, pay people to stand outside and pose this question to those leaving the theatre. And beat the sinners up afterwards. That would get rid of

which the theatre and Telemann are no longer two separate entities but one: THE WOMAN HAS NO CLOTHES ON. There is no alternative. Telemann feels he is approaching some kind of truth. Perhaps for the very first time in his career as a dramatist. The woman is naked and she opens a bottle of wine and pours herself a glass. Takes a hearty swig. Then she begins to busy herself rummaging through the cupboards. She gets down on all fours to reach the back of the cupboard. Where can the baking tin be? Where CAN it be? She has to stretch a bit more, her back arched, stretches, stretches, yes, there it is, get it out, onto the worktop, it has to be right on the other side of the island, a long way off, she bends over the worktop, has to get up on her toes to reach right across, stretches, stretches, on the tips of her toes, and a bit more, that's it, the tin's in the right position now. Writes Telemann. Then she has to go down on her knees again, she needs a bowl, a green plastic bowl, it has to go there, and then a ladle, also green, and into the fridge to get a chocolate mixture that has been cooling off, not much, just a little, it hasn't set yet, it can still be shaped, but it isn't runny, it just moves slowly, like lava, a bit faster than that though, Telemann writes, she stretches, back arched again, my, oh my, what a long way back the chocolate mixture is, she is almost there, stretches, there we are, onto the worktop with it. And now she needs something else, she rummages through the drawers, the cupboards, bends down, stretches, no, now she is hunting furiously, what is it she's after? She can't find it. Takes a despairing swig of wine. Looks disheartened. Writes Telemann. But now the theatre comes to an end. She is just standing there. We can't have that. Something has to happen. Someone has to come. A man comes! A man comes onto the stage. Who is this man? He seems familiar. He looks like Telemann. He looks very much like Telemann. Very, very much like Telemann. Has the man got clothes on? No clothes on? Telemann is embarrassed. The man has got clothes on, he writes. Underpants. Quite a smart pair of underpants. Nothing else.

Hello there!

Hello to you, too! Sorry to burst in on you, but the door was open and so I thought I'd better see if there was anything I could help with.

You came just at the right time.

Oh, good.

I can't find my tape measure.

You can't find your tape measure?

I've looked high and low and can't see it anywhere.

That's annoying.

Yes, it is. You see I'm making some chocolate thingies which have to be 19 to 20 centimetres long, but how can I do that if I haven't got a tape measure?

Mhm, that's awkward. Do you want me to nip out and buy you a tape measure?

No.

OK.

I'd prefer it if we, that is you and me, work out how long 19 to 20 centimetres is.

I see.

At this point Telemann pauses. He sips some wine and keeps the wine in his mouth, washing it from side to side and rolling it around his tongue sceptically. What is this all about? he thinks. It started as theatre and was theatre for quite a while, but now he fears it is beginning to turn into something else. But the theatre has many faces. Vulgar ones, too. So maybe this is still theatre, even though it is not painful to write it. Presumably it will become painful in due course. Telemann swallows. At any rate stopping now does not seem to be an option. The material will no doubt head in a less vulgar direction soon.

Can you suggest how we can work out how long 19 to 20 centimetres is?

No ... it ... no.

You haven't got something of about that length?

The woman looks at the man. Writes Telemann. Studies him. Then she looks down at the area covered by the scant underpants.

The man follows her gaze.

Have you?

Are you asking whether I know how long ...?

Yes.

It's a few years since I checked.

Yes, yes, but it doesn't change.

No.

It's not like your ears, or nose, which continue to grow throughout life.

No.

So if you knew before, you should know now.

Yes.

And how long was it before?

Last time I checked it was 19 to 20 centimetres.

Exactly the length these chocolate thingies I'm making should be! What a funny coincidence!

Yes. But I remember thinking it was difficult to know where to measure from.

I can well imagine that.

So depending on where I measured from it was sometimes 19 and sometimes 20 centimetres.

In an erect state?

Yes, it … certainly was.

Did you measure it from the very root, or what?

Yes, I suppose I must have done, but it's not so easy to say where the root starts.

Let's find out.

OK.

What's your name by the way?

Nothing.

Haven't you got a name?

I don't think we need names.

Alright then. Who needs names? Look at me now.

OK.

I don't quite know what you like, but if I stand like this, and a bit like this maybe, and put my hands here and lift them up like this, a bit towards you, and pout, does that have any effect?

Er … yes.

Goodness me! Mhm, nice. Well, I never. Would you mind if I hold it for a bit?

Not at all.

Now let me see … is it clean?

Yes, I think so.

Maybe we should give it a bit of a wash, just for safety's sake. After all, we *are* cooking.

Yes.

Let's just give it a rinse under the tap, there we go, and then I'll press it into the cake mixture, like so … and a bit more … there we are!

Right.

Well, thanks a lot for your help.

No problem.

The woman is about to let go, but doesn't after all. Writes Telemann. She looks at her hand and what it is holding. Her gaze meets his. And is this theatre? Or not? It's still a bit too early to say. A swig of wine.

Hey, I just had a thought.

What do you mean?

Well, I was thinking that while I'm here, holding you, I can feel quite a frisson, I have to confess, after all I'm not made of stone, and there's no great rush for the chocolate thingies, so ...

Oh, yes?

Well, what about if I grip you a bit tighter and, for instance, begin to move my hand backwards and forwards?

And?

Like this.

Yes.

Do you like it?

Yes, it's nice.

You like it?

Yes.

And what if I kneel down?

Why not?

Can you see that my head is now more or less at the same height as ... well... a part of your anatomy?

Yes.

How do you feel about that?

I think it's OK.

You think it's OK?

Yes.

I love putting things in my mouth, you know.

Yes.

I can't help myself.

Oh, yes.

And later I might scrabble onto the worktop on all fours.

I see.

How do you feel about that?

Sounds good.

Alternatively I can lie on my back.

Yes.

And then there's the cake mix.

Yes.

You can spread it all over and … am I beginning to talk too much?

A little bit maybe … since you ask.

Shall we just take things as they come?

I think so.

OK, then we'll just take our time.

But what about your husband?

My husband?

Yes.

Forget about him.

He's not going to come home any minute, is he?

Nononono. He's an art collector.

OK.

From dawn to dusk.

Oh, right.

He doesn't care anyway.

Are you sure?

He's not interested in real life.

OK.

That's enough about him.

Right.

Shall we get going then?

Yes, let's.

Are you ready?

I'm ready.

TELEMANN?!

Telemann!!

Are you still in there?

Open the door!

Telemann!!!

German, German, German, German, German, German, German?

German, German, German, German, German, Telemann, German, German, German, German.

German, German?

Bang! Bang!

German, German, German, German, German, German, German, German, German, Krankenhaus?

WHERE AM I?

Hi, Telemann! Good to see you've come round.

What happened?

We'll come to that later. Just rest for now.

German, German, German?

What is she saying?

She's asking if you're hungry.

No.

German.

Why am I in hospital?

Shall we leave that for later?

No.

Alright. You ... had a turn.

What kind of a turn?

We had to force the bathroom door open.

I see.

You were lying on the floor with your pants round your knees.

Right.

My toothbrush was soiled with one of your ... body fluids.

Was it?

Yes.

Sorry about that.

Yes.

I apologise.

Yes.

I'll buy you a new toothbrush.

Don't worry about it.

A new head at any rate.

Fine.

I'll do it today.

Thanks. Looked like you had been through the works.

It began with theatre.

Yes, I saw that.

Did you read it?

Yes.

Was it theatre?

To start with.

And then it stopped being theatre?

You could say that. The doctor says you had a minor stroke.

A stroke?

Yes. A transient ischaemic attack.

Thank you, I know what a TIA is.

The doctor says it can happen to anyone under great stress.

OK.

You seem to be alright again now though. You can come home. But the doctor says you should stop smoking.

No.

Yes, that's what he says.

You shouldn't listen to doctors.

Of course not.

I'm quite proud of the fact that I had a TIA.

Are you?

TIA is theatre.

Mhmm.

Nina?

Yes.

Come over here. I've got a surprise for you.

Have you?

Here you are.

What is it? Oh, a new toothbrush head.

Five of them actually.

So I see. Thanks a lot.

The least I could do.

Correct.

Do you think you'll be able to put what happened behind you?

Yes, I think so.

Good.

Were you thinking about her?

About whom?

Nigella.

I might have been. But it was theatre in a way. At least for quite a time. I wasn't myself. I was playing a role. That's what you do in theatre. You play roles.

I think you were yourself.
Do you?
Yes.
OK.

WHAT'S THIS WATCH DOING on my bedside table?

Which watch?

This Nazi watch.

I don't know.

Oh. It's not a present from you to me?

No.

OK.

Why do you call it a Nazi watch?

Because it's very accurate and also the style's a bit fancy.

I see.

But what's it doing here?

Perhaps it's Bader's.

Bader's?

Maybe.

Are you trying to say that Bader's personal belongings are on my bedside table?

That's how it would seem.

How come?

Goodness knows.

Has he been in here?

I think he said something about checking the central heating boiler.

But that's in the cellar.

Yes.

And, not only that, it's summer.

You're right.

This doesn't make sense.

No.

Have you got anything to tell me?

Yes and no.

WHAT! HAVE YOU BEEN to bed with Bader?

I suppose so.

Behind my back?

It was difficult to do it in any other way.

How incredibly brazen of you.

Do you think so?

Yes, I do.

Right.

Doing it is bad enough in the first place, but to do it with that blockhead Bader is really outrageous.

I can understand how you feel.

And you did it here?

Mostly.

Mostly? For crying out loud! Several times?

One thing led to another.

How many times?

I don't know.

How many?

Maybe seven.

Seven times?

Or maybe closer to a dozen. Or could be a bit more than that.

Are we talking a couple of dozen?

I think we are.

Bloody hell, Nina, I'll never get over you sleeping with Bader.

No. Just take the time you need.

But Bader? That dirty old bugger?

He's not much older than us.

Yes, he is.

Suppose so. But age is not so important when it comes to the crunch.

What is important then?

I don't know. We … Bader and I … speak the same language.

The same shit language!

Now, now, Telemann.

Nazi language!

Now, now.

WHAT ARE YOU THINKING about, Telemann?

What I'm thinking?

Yes.

I'm thinking you should go to hell.

I can see you're hurt.

Hurt? Go to hell!

It's not possible.

It's not possible?

No.

Because?

Because hell doesn't exist. It's just a word.

I don't want to see you. That's what it means.

OK. Never again? Or just for a while? Or what?

Have you finished with Bader?

Maybe not quite.

WHAT IS THAT SUPPOSED TO MEAN?

I don't know.

WHAT IS THAT SUPPOSED TO MEAN?

I'll have to work it out. I need some time alone to examine my feelings.

For Christ's sake, Nina, you're not seventeen any more, are you.

Maybe I am. In a way, I think we're all seventeen, and what's wrong with that?

I don't want to listen to this. I'm moving out.

You're moving out?

I'll find a room in the centre of the town.

Now, in the middle of the holiday?

Yes.

What about the children?

We'll have to have them a few days each, just like everyone else.

Who's going to have the car?

You.

HI, ME HERE.

Hi.

How are you?

OK. What about you?

Not so bad. What are you and the kids doing?

We're watching Heidi training. How about you?

I'm writing.

Good.

Yes.

Are you getting on OK in Bahnhofstrasse?

Fine. There's lots going on here. Bahnhofstrasse is never quiet. Or almost never.

Good.

Are you still seeing Bader?

Hey, this call is getting expensive.

Yes.

See you then.

Yes. Bye.

HI, IT'S ME AGAIN.

Hi.

I was thinking we could have something to eat together.

We've already eaten.

OK ... so all of you ... have eaten?

Yes.

In that case, I'll go down Bahnhofstrasse and find a takeaway.

Yes.

There's a big choice.

I'm sure there is.

And then I'll carry on writing.

Do that.

I'm making a lot of headway.

Good.

Bye then.

Bye.

Hi, it's me again.

I'm on my way out to get the kids.

That's exactly what I wanted to talk about.

Oh yes?

They don't want to.

They don't want to?

No.

Have you been …?

It's Heidi. She's very upset you've moved out.

Course she is. I take it you've explained the reason to them?

No. I don't think she needs to know anything.

Whoa there, Nina. Come onnn!

Don't say 'come on'.

So you want to make it seem as if I'm the problem, since it's me who's moved out?

All I'm saying is that the children don't want to stay with you.

This is heading for the law courts.

Pull yourself together, Telemann.

And you know me. I'm not the type to give up easily. You

can just dream about joint custody. I'm going to have the lot. Full custody. Just me. And you can see them every second weekend and every third Wednesday.

Calm down.

Calm down yourself.

Give them a bit of time. They have to get used to the situation. This is a long-term process.

I'm very sceptical about processes.

Yes, but it's a process nonetheless.

I hate processes.

TELEMANN, WHAT ABOUT MEETING, all five of us?

I didn't think the kids wanted to see me.

I've been speaking to them.

OK.

They need to see that you and I can talk.

I see.

And that we're still friends.

Right.

I suggest dinner.

Dinner's fine.

On neutral ground.

We're in Mixing Part Churches, remember. How neutral can it be?

You know what I mean.

I know what you mean.

MUM NEEDS A BIT of time to herself. And that's why I moved out.

Why time to yourself, Mum? And why did Dad move out and not you?

Tell her why, Nina.

I need time to think, Heidi.

Can't you think when Dad's around?

No.

Why not? I can think when Dad's around.

Good for you, Heidi.

This is not something you can understand at your age. It isn't meant for your ears anyway.

So I should accept the fact that you spend your time apart?

Actually, yes.

Weird.

Good, I think I'll have the pheasant.

You would.

What do you mean?

The pheasant costs three times as much as the other dishes, Nina. It even says so on the menu. Look here.

Surcharge for pheasant.

You do understand some German then?

Yes, I understand some German, and if I know you, and I do, then you're going to take it for granted the pheasant surcharge will be split between the two of us, even though I'm only having a sausage or two with sauerkraut, costing six euros.

We are a family after all.

I'm not going to pay any pheasant surcharge. Forget it.

Telemann, pull yourself together.

Me pull myself together? I'm not bloody paying the pheasant surcharge!

I think you should move back with us, Dad.

I AM NOT PAYING ANY BLOODY PHEASANT SURCHARGE!

IT'S ME.

Hi.

Sorry I lost my temper.

Yes.

It's not easy.

No.

Can you sleep?

I sleep well. How about you?

I don't sleep so well.

So what do you do?

I think about the theatre, and then I go out into Bahnhof-strasse and drink beer.

OK.

And I write as well.

You've been talking about doing some writing for ages.

Yes.

Good that something positive is coming out of this.

Yes. Are you seeing Bader?

Hey, this is getting expensive.

OK.

Good night.

Good night.

TELEMANN ISN'T WRITING. HE says he's writing, but he isn't. Everything has come to a halt for him. In fact, he finds being separated tough. He considers it theatre. All sudden changes are theatre. But he doesn't put it into practice. Instead he drinks beer and thinks about Nigella and at half past three in the morning he makes her chocolate honey cake (Divide the marzipan into 6 even pieces and shape them into fat, sausage-like bees' bodies, slightly tapered at the ends). He has put on seven kilos in as many days.

And then he masturbates. Quite a lot actually. Not something he goes around advertising, but nor is he ashamed of it. He thinks masturbation is theatre. In a way. All suppressed feelings are or can be theatre, thinks Telemann. It always begins with him reading through the start of his play. In an act of almost perfect self-delusion he plans to go through the text, editing and refining. But then he loses control. The buxom woman on the stage steals his thoughts and tragically his good intentions go up in smoke. Time after time. There is much, much more of it than many would consider seemly for a person of Telemann's age.

He wished some of the animal energy that clearly resides

in him could be used on the theatre. Such accursed luck. It is exactly what the theatre needs. The animal. The uncontrollable beast. Which sleeps when it is tired, and eats when it is hungry, and breeds when the urge makes itself felt, and which, if it is prevented from doing any of these things, goes on the attack, straight for the jugular.

Telemann's theatre, for the hundredth time, shouldn't be about how the family restricts the individual or proclaim that technology alienates man or that beneath the bourgeois surface lurk indescribable perversions. Telemann's theatre is to be pure energy. None of that clever stuff. Just energy. Dangerous energy. Come hell or high water.

Ring ring.

Hi, it's me.

Hi.

What are you doing?

I'm writing.

Good.

And then I was wondering whether to nip down to the bierstube. They've got a Nazi quiz every Wednesday.

You're so childish.

Certainly am.

I hate it.

Hate is a strong word.

It's the manner in which you are childish that I am allergic to.

Do you think so?

Yes.

OK. What are you doing?

I've just put the children to bed.

OK ... and ... have you ...?

Don't ask about Bader.

OK.

My doctor needs a sample of your skin.

What?

He says he can develop a vaccine so that I can tolerate you better.

Does he?

Yes. But he needs a few molecules or something from you.

Do you feel a need to tolerate me then?

Yes, I do. We're bound to have a lot to do with each other for many more years to come.

But have you ... are you?

Don't ask about Bader.

OK.

He's in Hindenburgstrasse.

OK.

The doctor, I mean. Number 8.

OK.

Doktor Engels.

I see. Is he a young doctor?

No.

Old?

Yes, basically.

You don't know if he's had any experience of selection procedures?

Grow up!

Because, if so, I'm a bit dubious.

Seriously, Telemann.

Was there any Nazi memorabilia in his surgery?

Telemann!

It's FIVE O'CLOCK IN the morning and Telemann is reading Nigella's *Feast*. She writes that she knows you can frighten men off by cooking for them, but still reckons there is no harm done with a frisky plate of pasta she and the lucky man can gorge on in the middle of the night. She has taken the idea from Nora Ephron's book *Heartburn*, she says. The first time a man and a woman spend the night together, after a few hours of lovemaking, spaghetti alla carbonara fits the bill perfectly, and if there's any left, there's nothing like working up an appetite. What a dizzying thought, Telemann thinks.

He reads the extract once, twice, he reads it three and four and five times, picking out bits of the text and examining every single statement from several different angles. He deconstructs the text, in fact, just like in his student days, he remembers, but quickly decides that reminiscing must be jettisoned. Reminiscing is theatre, true enough, but it is old-fashioned theatre, out with it. Telemann is drunk. And has just eaten about 30 chocolate caramel crispy cakes that an inner female voice ordered him to make a couple of hours ago. He stirred the cornflakes in the chocolate mixture with the spatula until they were all well covered. It was only with the greatest difficulty that he managed to let them stand in the fridge on a little tray or a big plate for at least an hour. Meanwhile he got stuck into some alcohol and ordered *Heartburn* from Amazon.

There are three particular aspects of Nigella's carbonara recipe that he seizes on. First of all, there was the bit about guzzling the food in bed. And then the bit about him staying at yours all night. And finally the bit about working up an appetite afterwards. There was nothing else; the latter could only be interpreted as an absolutely shamelessly undisguised invitation. First of all, they keep at it until three o'clock and then Nigella disappears into the kitchen for half an hour and returns with a giant pan of spaghetti carbonara. Then they're at it again. And then the leftovers have to be eaten. And after that what else can they do but carry on. It's a never-ending cycle of copulation and carbonara. Bang, bang, bang. Off she goes, into the kitchen, carbonara, carbonara, bang, bang. Fantastic. How many times has this happened? How many all-night first dates has she had? Two? One for each husband? But what about her earlier relationships? Bloody hell! It must have happened 30 or 40 times. Telemann is sure of this. He paces the floor of the tiny room in Bahnhofstrasse. And what about Saatchi? Jews don't eat bacon. At least not usual Jews. But maybe Saatchi is a bit different. Perhaps that was what she fell for. That he is an unusual Jew. That must have made the situation extra exciting for both of them. Yuk! The dirty bugger!

Telemann opens another bottle of wine.

Pen and paper. After all, an old-fashioned letter makes a greater impression than an email. Not to mention a text message. A letter has to be taken seriously.

How can I say this to you?

My darling, where to start?

Please read this!

Please read this, Nigella, please!

I am not just another fan. Please continue reading.

Meet me outside Wembley Stadium at five o'clock on August 1st. (Wembley? So stupid but where else could he suggest? He ought to have travelled to London a lot more, but of course Nina always wanted to go to Nazi Germany. Sod it!) *I am a Norwegian dramatist (big word, I know), a few years younger than yourself. A few years younger than your pretty self?* Jesus! But age is his strongest suit. In addition to the theatre. Nigella needs a younger man. It is on her mind day and night. But she's caught. She can't say so without hurting Saatchi's feelings. He's more than sixteen years older than her. A difference of that kind is exciting when the man is thirty-five or forty, but not when he is getting on for seventy. Nigella wants out. Maybe she also wants more children. *I am fertile and can easily give you children. One child? Two? It's up to you.* When is it that women can't have any more children? Hm.

Maybe I should be more forthright: I can save you from Saatchi. Please continue to read! I know that you hate your husband. That's OK. Don't be ashamed. Let the hatred embrace you (Can you say that?) I am love. Hell, no. Thank you for the music. Music? She'll understand that I'm talking about food. Music as a metaphor for food. Why not? She must be ravenous for metaphors after living with such a dry old stick as Saatchi.

Dearest Nigella. Thank you for the music. That's a perfect start. Please continue reading. I can save you. 4 ever.

Ding dong.

What?

Ding dong.

Who's that?

Who do you think?

It's not the most convenient time.

Hurry up, Telemann. We're all here.

Oh, alright.

Are you going to open up?

OK.

Hi.

What a mess you look!

Do I?

Hi, Dad.

Hi, Heidi.

Hi.

Hi Berthold.

Hi Dad.

Hi Sabine.

What are you doing?

Not a lot.

Didn't you sleep last night?

Not quite sure. Maybe I didn't.

Weren't we supposed to be going to Zugspitze?

Again?

The children want to show you it.

Do they really?

Yes.

We've already talked about this, Telemann.

Have we?

We talked about it last night.

Was it an OK conversation?

Fairly.

Good. You must excuse the mess. I think I've got some chocolate caramel crispy cakes for you. And maybe some carbonara, over there on the bedside table.

We've just had breakfast.

Yes, of course.

Dad?

Yes.

Why does it say Nigella on the wall?

It … it … was there before I arrived. The rent's cheap,

you know, furnished … and … you see, with writing on the wall. I think it's some kind of German custom or habit. Is that not so, Nina? They write on the walls quite a lot down here, don't they?

What?

Make of it what you will. It's probably been there since the war.

Are you coming or what?

Erm, maybe you should go without me. So I can think about the theatre and get some sleep?

I think you should come with us. What's this?

It's theatre.

Looks like a letter to me.

But it's theatre.

I think it's a letter.

It's theatre.

I see.

What about Bader?

What about him?

Is he going to Zugspitze?

No.

OK.

Are you coming, Dad?

Maybe.

FANTASTIC VIEW.

It is, isn't it.

Certainly is. Absolutely fantastic. View.

Look, Dad!

Yeah, fantastic.

There's Austria.

Wow, is that what it looks like?

It looks like a wonderful country.

Take it easy, Telemann.

I'm hungry. Do you think they've got a Fritzl Schnitzel by the cable car station?

Get a grip!

Me get a grip?

Yes.

Me get a grip?

Yes.

You need to get a grip.

I'll get a grip as well.

You mean we should both get a grip?

Yes.

So the next question is: how's it going with you and Ba…?

Don't.

Don't what?

Not in front of the children.

What are you two going on about?

Nothing, Heidi.

Do you think I'm stupid?

No.

We just want you to concentrate on your tennis. If you're focussed you might beat Anastasia later today.

I'll never beat her.

What a negative attitude.

That's got shit-all to do with you.

Of course you'll beat her.

No, I won't.

If you have mental poise you'll beat her.

And I won't have unless you tell me what's going on.

No.

That only makes me twice as keen to know what's going on.

I quite understand.

This is something only grown-ups can understand, Heidi. Dad and I want to keep it to ourselves and you should respect that.

You can tell me, Dad, can't you?

I'm actually wondering whether I should.

Don't!

Go on, Dad.

If I do, it's to teach Heidi that mental poise is overrated. Which players lose their mental poise is of very little interest. Take John McEnroe, for example. Zero poise and still the best. Mental poise in the theatre is death. It's death.

See, Mum.

Now I'm going to tell her.

No, don't!

Heidi, your mother is having a relationship with Bader. That's the bottom line.

Yukky!

Yes, it is, isn't it. Horrible, don't you think?

I just can't believe you told her!

Yuk.

I can't believe it!

But did they … did they …?

You can bet your life they did. A couple of dozen times. Presumably more. Who knows?

Yuk.

I agree.

I'm lost for words, Telemann.

Same here. Fantastic view. Austria and all that. What a country!

Hɪ, ɪᴛ's ᴍᴇ.

Hi.

Heidi's on her way over to you.

Is she?

She doesn't want to be with me any more.

OK.

Is that all you've got to say?

Basically, yes. I understand her. I don't want to live with you, either.

Look, now I think you're getting … you're getting …

I think you should keep quiet.

You think *I* should keep quiet?

Yes, how did the tennis match go?

Heidi won.

Do you understand the significance of that?

No, Telemann, what is it?

It means you should keep your mouth shut, Nina. Tightly shut. And what's more, you can stuff Bader and his Schneeberg eggs, and the hens too for that matter, where the sun never shines. By the way, it'd be best to blind the hens first. Use a sharp instrument, jab it into their eyes, maybe it's a bit difficult the first few times, but then you'll get used to it, and after that you can serve Bader eggs from hens which once saw snow-capped mountains and now can't see anything.

You're sick, Telemann.

OK.

You're sick.

True.

DAD?

Yes.

Nigella wasn't on the wall when you moved in.

Wasn't she?

No.

You mean I wrote it?

Yes.

You could well be right.

Are you in love with her?

It's more complicated than that.

How do you mean?

It has facets and aspects that fourteen-year-olds might not understand.

Do you think she's sexy?

I don't wish to comment on that.

Why not?

It would be too superficial. When you're young the world is black and white, but the older you get, the more shades and nuances you see.

Eh?

Appearance is just a façade, Heidi. You have to look behind and beyond it. Into the very stuff of life.

I think I'll move back with Mum.

OK.

Don't stop reading!

Meet me outside the Globe Theatre. July 28th. At five pm. Telemann has never understood the difference between am and pm, but he can wait there early in the morning and in the afternoon, he thinks. No, not bloody likely. Not at five o'clock in the morning. *Let's say half past nine. PM. And just as Shakespeare could see through people* (smart to mention Shakespeare) *I can see right through you. I know you are desperate. I know that your TV programmes and books are cries for help. You want someone to come and rescue you. I am that person.*

And I hate art. No.

You know that beautiful feeling of being seen and understood? Prepare to live with that feeling for the rest of your life. Maybe you can wear that pale blue and green sweater of yours, the thin one, or whatever you want of course, but that sweater is nice. I just mentioned it in case you wonder what I like. But I like everything about you, so don't worry. Here is a photograph of me, so that you can recognise me. I have been called handsome, but … so … I wonder what you think. Anyway, it is how we are on the inside that matters. I will be holding a punnet of strawberries (extremely pleased with this). If you want, I can move to London. No problem. Since I am a dramatist (big word, but still) I can work anywhere as long as there is an internet connection. Hell, I can even work without an internet connection. And I think that your kids and my kids will instantly like each other. Kids are kids. Aren't they? And I like carbonara.

Perfect.

Hi, Nina, it's me. Did I wake you up?

Yes.

Good. How do you say 'stamp' in German?

It's four o'clock in the morning, Telemann.

I know.

Can we talk later?

No.

How do you say 'stamp'?

Briefmarke.

Thank you.

Are you going to send a letter now?

Work that one out for yourself. Thank you again.

Hi.

Hello there, princess.

Have you come to see the match?

Yes.

Have you been waiting long?

I didn't know exactly when you would be playing, but I haven't got much else on … so this … was just very nice. I've been thinking about the theatre.

I don't know if you're allowed to drink here.

Nor me.

How fat you've got, Dad.

No, I haven't.

Yes, you have.

Anyway, as opposed to what you believe, we need fat. Especially if people, like me, are working in the theatre. The brain is one big lump of fat. If you starve yourself you can't write theatre.

But when your waistline starts expanding maybe it's a sign you're eating too much.

That's just a myth. As I said, you have to learn to analyse and see things at a deeper level. Otherwise you will continue to be easy prey to sensational journalism. You have to see behind the façade, Heidi. Behind. And behind again. As far into and behind as at all possible. You're missing the boat. While you play tennis other fourteen-year-olds are beginning to see behind the façade. Soon you'll be seriously behind. You'll be standing there with your pockets full of tennis balls wondering where it all went wrong.

Mum says you're depressed.

I'm sure she does.

Are you?

Far from it.

Sure?

Course I'm sure. Mum says so many strange things. Don't listen to her.

Shouldn't I?

Absolutely not. The trick is to pretend you're listening but not to take any notice of what she says.

OK.

That's the best advice I can give you.

Thank you.

You need to break free, Heidi.

Do you think so?

There's no doubt about it. And to help you on your way I can tell you something about her you don't know.

Go on then.

You know how she usually spends quite a long time in the bathroom in the morning?

Yes.

And just as much time in the bathroom before she goes to bed.

Yes.

What do you think she's up to?

I thought she was putting her face on and taking it off.

Well, there's something else she does.

What's that?

She puts things up her bum.

What?

She likes to put things up her bum.

What sort of things?

Any old small object. Batteries, marbles, once there was even a golf ball.

Yuk.

There are all sorts in this world. Some like one thing, others like something else. Your mother puts things up her bum. You have to accept that.

How disgusting!

Yeah, well, it took me a few years to get used to it, but now I don't think about it much any more.

But it's awful!

I don't think you should be so hasty to judge her, Heidi. Give it some thought for a couple of days. Let it sink in. And by the way I don't think you should tell her you know. She'll only deny it and then we're back where we started. Oh well. Now you know at least. So you can keep it in mind.

186 | ERLEND LOE

COME ON, HEIDI! BEAT THE HELL OUT OF IT! YEAH, THAT'S THE WAY! UNSTOPPABLE! TERRIFIC! SERVE DOWN THE LINE!

Maybe you could calm down a little?

Am I making too much noise?

Yes.

And what makes that any of your business?

I just think we should let our daughters get on with the game.

Do you know what I think?

No.

I think you don't like it when my daughter beats your daughter.

And I think you've put on some weight.

Yes, but I don't think she cares.

Who?

The man she's married to now was quite fat when they met. But she still married him.

Who?

The art collector. I'm not even close to being as fat as him, so I don't think she'd have any objection to marrying me, either.

Have you been drinking?

Although marriage is not really what I'm after.

I have no idea what you're talking about.

Is your husband fat?

I'm not going to answer that.

I think he's fat.

Whatever.

I think he's huge. And you could do with a bit more fat on you, too. You have a nice face, but some more fat here wouldn't go amiss. And maybe around here.

Get your hands off me.

And if I don't?

I'll call security.

Right. Call the Nazi security.

You're insane.

FANTASTIC, HEIDI! BLOODY TERRIFIC! HEIDI! HEIDI! HEIDI! HEIDI! HEIDI!

Hello?

What on earth has got into you?

What's got into me?

Heidi says you were drunk at the tennis match.

I totally reject that allegation.

And then you said I liked putting things up my bum.

It's difficult to hear what you're saying, Nina.

There are limits.

Poor connection, pip-pip-pip-achtung-achtung.

Seriously, Telemann!

Nina, this is getting expensive.

Telemann!

H<small>I, IT'S ME</small>.

Hi.

What a strange dialling tone!

Oh yes.

As if you were in a different country.

A different country?

Yes.

Which country might that be?

I've no idea.

In a way, Germany's a different country.

Yes. But you're not in a different, different country, are you?

Oh no. I'm in Bahnhofstrasse, as usual. That's where I live.

Telemann, I think we need to meet, just you and me, to talk things over.

Can't.

Why not?

I'm … working.

Can't you squeeze in a meeting?

No. I'm so deep into the play, I am the play, so to speak, and that fills my world.

So I don't exist?

In a way, no.

But I do exist, Telemann.

Of course, of course. But there are different layers here. As in the theatre. Layer upon layer.

Train approaching Paddington Station! Paddington! Platform on the right hand side!

What was that?

What was what?

Paddington?

What about Paddington?

Are you in London?

How can I be in London?

You are in London!

This is getting expensive, Nina.

What are you doing in London?

WHERE CAN YOU BUY strawberries in this town? And where the hell is the Shakespeare Theatre? Nigella is probably already waiting there. She can't let this chance slip. Last night she said her goodbyes. Saatchi, the little whiner, must have started crying and had to be consoled and patted to sleep. Keep the house, she said. Bloody hell. Telemann laughs. What's the use of fame and fortune when you lose the love of your life? Nothing. It's theatre. Merciless. Then she dashed off in her thin blue sweater and has been wandering around in the town in a state of suspense ever since. She is filled with expectation. Her body is shaking uncontrollably. Convulsions. A new start. Whoever would have imagined this would happen to me, she thinks, to little old me! There's a fruit store. Strawberries! Please! Here. Thanks. Tube. Change at Baker Street, then to Bond Street, Green Park, Westminster, God, it's getting late, Waterloo and off at London Bridge. And out. Out! Where is this Globe? There! There! But where's Nigella? Isn't she here? Is that possible? Telemann paces up and down. Eating strawberries. That must mean the wrangling has gone on all night. Saatchi wouldn't let her go. He couldn't accept the defeat. He is nothing without her. I can't go on without you! You have to! Nooooo! Stay here a little longer. Does he hit her? Does Saatchi become violent? Heavens above. Saatchi hits her. Telemann has no time to lose. Run, run, run. Look at the map, look at the map, what a complicated town. Excuse me, where is Eaton Square? Thanks. Waterloo, Westminster, change trains, on to St James' Park, off at Victoria. More running. What impressive houses. Which number is hers? Is it this one? Ding dong. Wait. Blink. Yes? Nigella? Over there, sir. Thanks. You're welcome. Run. Ding dong. Yes? Tell her Telemann is here. The lady is not to be disturbed, sir. Is he beating her? I beg your pardon? Is he beating her? Goodbye, sir. Thank you, sir. Door bangs. Shit. Saatchi has got the butler on his side. Good cop, bad cop. One is pleasant with her to get her to talk, the other one beats her. Telemann hides in the bushes. Jumps as high as he can to see through the windows. Did he see her hair? She's alive! Nigella! Thank God, she's alive. Merciful God! Nigella! Nigella!

Hello, sir.

I'm glad you came, Officers. Saatchi's beating her.

Will you please leave the premises, sir?

You must arrest the Jew!

Come with us, sir.

Please arrest the Jew!

We won't ask you nicely again, sir.

Hɪ.

Hi.

Shall we meet?

I thought you were working.

Yes, I was, but now I've put it aside for a bit.

I see.

Where would you like to meet?

It's you who wants us to meet.

Yes, but a few days ago it was you who wanted to meet.

So now you're ringing me because you think I want to meet you?

Yes.

But it's not very important for you to meet?

I wouldn't say that. We can meet.

If you don't want to meet me, then there's no point!

Nina? ... Nina?

Hɪ, ɪᴛ's ᴍᴇ ᴀɢᴀɪɴ.

Yes?

We got off on the wrong foot before. I want to meet you. I need to meet you.

OK.

What about just going to the cinema?

Fine by me.

If Heidi can look after the other two, we could go to Munich and see a film.

What kind of film?

I can see here that the arts cinema in Munich is showing a Hungarian film tonight.

Uhuh?

Satan's Tango.

That's a strange title.

Yes.

Be a bit like the old days. Just you and me. In the cinema.

Yes.

THIS IS GREAT, NINA. Us two, driving from Mixing Part Churches to Munich to see a film. I like that.

It's not called Mixing Part Churches.

Yes, it is.

Maybe we should take it in turns to drive?

No way. I've had a few beers.

What were you doing in London?

I haven't been to London.

Can't you just come clean?

I've just been writing. Theatre.

I heard on the phone that you were on a train.

No, you didn't!

Telemann!

I was listening to *The Sounds of London*.

The Sounds of London?

A CD I bought in Bahnhofstrasse.

It makes me sick to think you can lie to me without the slightest compunction.

If we begin to compare lies you won't come out of this very well, Nina.

It makes me sick.

You're not the only one.
I beg your pardon.
Who feels sick.
But it really makes me sick.
Same here.

How LONG DOES THIS film last?

Seven and a half hours.

Are you kidding?

No.

But it's already revolting. Fat, miserable people wandering around in the mud and rain doing God knows what. And that little girl torturing the cat.

Yes. And later on she kills the cat and herself, too.

Have you seen this film before?

Yep. And when she's dead there's a helluva long scene which, time-wise, actually precedes the scene where the girl dies, where they dance and drink in the café while a beardy talks about something a person called Jerimias said.

You're sick in the head!

You need to see this, Nina.

No, I don't.

Yes, you do. Nothing comes close to this. It's theatre. Even if it's a film.

You're sick, Telemann!

Maybe. But that's exactly what the film's about. You and me and Bader and all the others. And our condition. The sick human condition. And the nastiness of it all.

I want to go home.

To Mixing Part Churches?

I want to go home, Telemann. I just want to go home.

Out of the question. Do you realise how rarely this film is shown? This is a unique opportunity. Let's see a bit more. Just a couple of hours. Two or three hours.

Hi, it's me.

Hi.

Thanks for yesterday.

My pleasure.

It was an unusual film.

It was, wasn't it. Plenty of food for thought, eh?

Mhm. What are you doing?

What do you think?

Writing?

Correct. Theatre. What are you doing?

Telemann, I was thinking we could go back home today.

Oh yes.

And I wanted to say that …

Yes?

I'm not allergic to you after all.

Aren't you?

No.

Are you over it?

Yes.

But were you really allergic to me for a while or was it just something you said?

It was just something I said.

Hm. I see. Actually, I think that's quite titillating.

Do you think?

It gives you an air of mystery and inscrutability.

Really?

Important theatrical attributes, both of them.

Right.

Exciting.

Does that mean you're coming back with us then?

I'm not quite sure.

I think you should come.

What about Bader?

He's staying here. It's finished.

Finished?

Yes.

Great.

Are you coming home then?

Maybe.

I'VE BEEN SO STUPID, Telemann.

Yes, you have.

So incredibly stupid.

I quite agree. And Bader's stupid.

Yes, he is stupid.

Both of you are stupid.

Yes.

And not a little stupid, either.

No.

Extremely stupid.

Yes. Kiss me.

We'll leave that for a while.

OK.

And Mixing Part Churches is stupid.

Yes.

And next year we'll go to London.

Yes.

But I'm not stupid, am I.

No.

But you're stupid?

Yes.

That's alright then. Good to get that straight.

Yes.

We'll forget all about it then, Nina.

Oh, Telemann!

But I hope you understand that I'll have to mention Bader if we have any arguments or if I feel you are being unreasonable or don't let me think about the theatre as much as I need to.

Fine.

I'd also like to have the right to threaten you with mentioning Bader if I feel the situation demands it.

OK, but not for ever.

For a year?

Alright.

Or maybe a bit more.

Let's wait and see.

Good. Now you can have a kiss if you want.

Yes please.

There!

Hi, Dad!

Hi, kids. Good to see you. Shall we head for home?

Yes!

What do you say to a final Nazi ice cream?

Hurrah!

Would you like an ice cream too, Nina?

Yes, I would.
One of those Nazi cornets?
Yes, please.

ARE THE KIDS ASLEEP?
Yes.
Where are we?
We'll soon be in Hamburg.
Wasn't it razed to the ground?
It was rebuilt after the war.
Blimey.

WHAT ARE YOU GOING to do about the surplus kilos?

Nothing.

Nothing?

Nothing.

I read that that fella, Nigella's husband, what's his name again?

Saatchi.

He's lost 25 kilos.

Has he now?

Just by eating eggs. Three for breakfast, three for lunch and three for supper. For months.

Prat.

They say he feels a lot better now.

No doubt.

Perhaps that would be an idea for you.

No way. In fact, I've been thinking about eating to my heart's content, letting myself go and becoming as fat as a pig.

I don't think that's a good idea.

I know.

Don't do it, Telemann.

You won't recognise me.
No.
Fat people are theatre.
Mhm.
Obesity is theatre.
Really?

TELEMANN?

Yes.

Do you think we've learnt anything?

In Mixing Part Churches, do you mean?

Yes.

No.

Nothing?

No.

How sad.

It's not sad.

Yes, it is. I think it is.

I hate people who learn from their mistakes.

Give it a break.

And people who understand and see the error of their ways and acknowledge all manner of things. We are what we are, *basta*. That's why theatre exists.

Is that why?

Yes.

You're theatre, Nina.

Am I?

Yes.

What about you?

I'm theatre, too.

And Bader?

There's more theatre in Bader than you and me put together.

I see.

When I get home I'm going to put this down on paper and write off all the expenses against tax.

Are you?

Too bloody right I am. And I'll use some of the money to buy a thin, light blue sweater for you.

Like the one Nigella has?

Yes. And maybe a punnet of strawberries.

WHERE ARE WE NOW?

    We're close to Kiel.

    Wasn't that destroyed?

    They've rebuilt it.

    Kiel too?

    Yes.

    I'm mute with admiration.

WELL, THANKS FOR A nice holiday, Telemann.

Thank you, too.

All in all, it was pretty good, wasn't it?

Mhm.

What with the mountains … and …

Yes.

But do you know what?

No.

Sleeping with Bader didn't give me anything.

Didn't it?

No.

I'm pleased to hear that.

It didn't give me anything at all.

Good.

But I pretended it was good.

Did you?

Yes.

Hell's bells, Nina! That's theatre. That's what I call theatre. Bugger me. Serves him right. The dirty old bastard.

Yes.

Serves him right, doesn't it?

Yes.

Bloody hell, Nina. That's what I call theatre.